LOOKING AT THE

INVISIBLE UNIVERSE

BOOKS BY JAMES JESPERSEN AND JANE FITZ-RANDOLPH

Time and Clocks for the Space Age
Mercury's Web
Rams, Roms and Robots
From Quarks to Quasars
Looking at the Invisible Universe

A photo of the Southern Hemisphere sky showing the Large and Small Magellanic clouds and the star Achernar.

LOOKING AT THE
INVISIBLE UNIVERSE

By James Jespersen & Jane Fitz-Randolph

Illustrated with diagrams
by Bruce Hiscock and with photographs

ATHENEUM   1990   NEW YORK

PHOTO CREDITS
AIP—Niels Bohr Library 28, 35 (Margrethe Bohr Coll.); 44 (Research Corp.); 45
(AT&T Bell Labs.); 98 (E. Scott Barr Coll.); 132 (Palomar Observatory); 136
(Physics Today Coll.)
Edison National Historic Site 58
David E. Fisher 46
Harvard Observatory 2, 40, 85
Jet Propulsion Lab. 115, 117, 119, 120a (David Smalls), 120b
Adair P. Lane (Boston University) and John Bally (AT&T Bell Labs.) 65
NASA 74
New York Public Library 3, 112

Text copyright © 1990 by James Jespersen and Jane Fitz-Randolph
Illustrations copyright © 1990 by Bruce Hiscock

Atheneum
Macmillan Publishing Company
866 Third Avenue, New York, NY 10022
Collier Macmillan Canada, Inc.
First Edition
Printed in the United States of America
10 9 8 7 6 5 4 3 2 1
Designed by Kimberly M. Hauck

Library of Congress Cataloging-in-Publication Data
Jespersen, James.
    Looking at the invisible universe / by James Jespersen and Jane
Fitz-Randolph; illustrated with diagrams by Bruce Hiscock and with
photographs.—1st ed.   p.   cm.
Bibliography: p.   Includes index.
Summary: Discusses the aspects of our universe that we do not see
and how they were discovered.
ISBN 0-689-31457-4
1. Cosmology—Juvenile literature. [1. Cosmology. 2. Astronomy.
3. Physics.] I. Fitz-Randolph, Jane. II. Hiscock, Bruce, ill.
III. Title. QB983.J48 1990 520—dc20 89-14998 CIP AC

Contents

LOOKING AT THE
INVISIBLE UNIVERSE

1

Questions, Questions

Some of nature's ways are open and straightforward, easy to observe. Others are so puzzling and bizarre that it's hard to believe the results of careful experiments devised to study them. Some questions about nature seem too simple to ask. Others are so hard to answer that scientists argue over them for decades, even centuries. Scientists are often fascinated by questions that seem too trivial or uninteresting to the average person to think about. This is because the scientists see implications in the questions that others cannot appreciate.

The British philosopher Alfred North Whitehead said, "It requires a very unusual mind to undertake the analysis of the obvious." One characteristic of such a mind is a relentless examination of a problem from every conceivable perspective. A peculiar curiosity drives such investigators to set aside apparent or traditional concepts about things and keep probing with observations and questions that others discard or overlook.

Some of the world's most distinguished scientists have

thought about problems this way, and often asking some of the simplest questions has provoked some of the greatest changes in our understanding of the universe. Isaac Newton questioned why an apple plunges toward Earth while the moon stays suspended in the sky; his wondering led him to his universal law of gravitation. Einstein questioned why objects of different weights—a golf ball and a cannonball, for example—fall to the ground together; his wondering set him on the path toward his general theory of relativity, a theory some scientists consider the most commanding solitary intellectual achievement of all time.

Small children, starting usually at about age two, are noted for asking countless questions—questions that perplex and too often annoy adults: Why is the sky blue? Why do stars twinkle? Where does the sun go at night? Certainly one of the commonest and easiest observations in astronomy—one that even two-year-olds make nearly every day—is that night follows day. When it occurs to them to ask why this is so, some adult—or perhaps an older and therefore wiser child—gives them the obvious answer that we've all accepted ever since *we* were two years old: The sun is shining on the other side of the world.

A globe of Earth helps with this explanation. The side facing the sun is bathed in light, while Earth itself cuts off this light on the side away from the sun. As our concepts of astronomy become a little more sophisticated, we learn that the stars are suns similar to our own sun, some of them many times larger. But they are so far away that they appear to be only points of light in the vast darkness.

The observation and its explanation seem so obvious and logical that it's hard to imagine that anyone ever questioned them, much less a scientist. Yet this simple observation—that night follows day—is at the heart of a question so profound that scientists have puzzled over it for hundreds of years and have been able to find a satisfactory answer only in our own century: Why is the night sky dark?

One thinker bothered by this question that seems to most persons too simple to think about was a nineteenth-century German physician named Wilhelm Olbers. Olbers was as full of questions as a two-year-old; and like many other educated men of his time, he made important discoveries outside his chosen profession. A talented amateur mathematician as well as astronomer, he made the first accurate determination of the orbits of comets. From these calculations he was the first to realize that comets are born in a kind of celestial junkyard on the outskirts of the solar system. He also discovered that asteroids come from a belt of debris lying between the orbits of Mars and Jupiter. One subject that interested him deeply was the problem of day dissolving into night, and we know him best for "Olbers' paradox."

Wilhelm Olbers asked, "Where's the light?"

In 1823 Olbers wrote a paper, "On the Transparency of Space," in which he speculated on the problem of why the sky, both day and night, is not infinitely bright at every point. The reason for his puzzlement is really not hard to understand if we accept Newton's view of the universe, as most educated persons of Olbers' century did. There was good reason to have almost divine belief in Newton's views. Before Newton, the motion of everything from billiard balls to the most distant planets was a mystery; after Newton, the mystery was seen as a natural part of the majestic and logical plan of "the maker of us all." In a handful of laws, Newton had summed up almost every scientific observation known to humans.

The stage for Newton's laws of motion and gravitation was a universe extending without end in time and space. This infinite universe was everywhere governed by the same laws and contained a uniform distribution of stars much like our own sun. The idea that the stellar distribution had to be uniform was a natural consequence of Newton's own law of gravitation. If some part of the universe had a greater density of stars than another, then slowly but surely, because of the pull of gravity, that denser part would attract nearby stars to its neighborhood, magnifying the density imbalance. Thus the imbalance would grow without end until every star in the universe ended up at the initial point of density imbalance. Since the universe is obviously not one compact mass sitting in the midst of infinite space, the only conclusion is that stars are evenly distributed to maintain the delicate balance of gravitational force necessary to support a uniform stellar distribution.

The thing that puzzled Olbers, given Newton's delicate balance, was the question, Where is the light from all these stars? In his paper, Olbers reasoned from two scientific facts: Imagine, he said, that Earth is the center of an infinite number of shells, each of the same thickness (Figure 1). The volume of space enclosed by each shell, as the figure shows, increases with its distance from Earth. A shell centered at one billion light-years from Earth encloses less space than a shell centered at two billion light-years. (One light-year is the distance light travels in one year.) That was the first fact of Olbers' argument. The second pointed out that the brightness of a star decreases as its distance from Earth increases.

fig. 1

Now we have two competing effects: The light contributed by stars from more distant shells is weaker than the light contributed by stars in nearby shells because the stars in the more distant shells are farther away. But the more distant shells contain more stars. Olbers was able to show, using simple geometry, that these two competing effects exactly offset each other, so that any shell contributes just as much light at Earth's location as any other shell. That is, the loss in light intensity from stars in more distant shells is exactly compensated for by the fact that the more distant shells contain just enough more stars to make up for this loss.

With Earth at the center of an infinite number of shells each contributing the same amount of light, and with each star beaming its light in all directions from its fixed point in the universe throughout eternity, the whole sky, both day and night, should be infinitely bright. Darkness, after all, is not something that either blocks or absorbs light; darkness is simply the absence of light. But how could there be an absence of light anywhere in the universe Newton described? This is Olbers' paradox: If the universe is infinite and has a uniform distribution of stars, where's the light?

Olbers' own explanation was that some unknown interstellar matter absorbs the light from the most distant stars, so that Earth is bathed only in light from neighboring stars. But we now know that's not the answer. Light is just another form of energy; so if it were absorbed by some sort of interstellar matter, that matter would eventually heat up and start radiating light just as the coiled element of an electric stove glows when it is hot. So the light from the distant stars would still reach Earth, although indirectly. In Chapter 3 we shall investigate in some detail the relationship between the temperature of a body and the light it gives off. This relationship is a basic key to understanding the structure and contents of the universe.

When someone is so bogged down in the details of an undertaking that he loses track of the original goal, we say he can't see the forest for the trees. A partial solution to Olbers' paradox can be found in a kind of reverse version of this old saying: We can't see the trees for the forest. When we stand in the middle of a forest with a uniform distribution of trees that are all more or less the same size, there is a certain distance beyond which we can no longer see individual trees. The reason is simple. Beyond some distance, no matter in which direction we look, there will always be one or more trees blocking our view of the

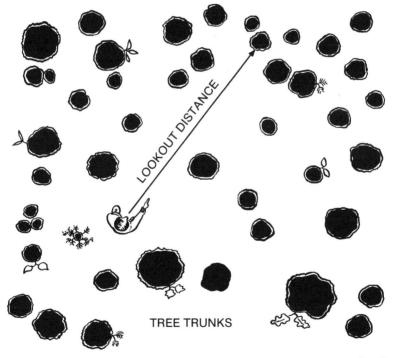

TREE TRUNKS

fig. 2

trees beyond. This distance, the lookout distance, depends on the density of the trees and their average trunk size. If the forest is large enough, there will always be a lookout distance, no matter how small or sparsely scattered the trees. See Figure 2.

An infinite universe with a uniform distribution of stars also has a lookout distance. That is, in any direction there will always be stars whose light does not reach us because it is blocked by closer, intervening stars. This blockage helps to explain why the sky is not *infinitely* bright: Shells of stars beyond the lookout distance do not contribute to the light reaching Earth. But this partial solution to the problem of why the night sky is not infinitely bright in an infinite universe does not explain why the sky is *dark* at night.

Although we attach Olbers' name to the paradox of the dark nighttime sky, he was not the first to puzzle over it. An Englishman, Thomas Digges, a firm supporter of Copernicus, wrote about the problem in 1576. Until the time of Copernicus, the world generally accepted Aristotle's belief that the universe was finite, unchanging, and that Earth stood at its center. Copernicus greatly simplified astronomical mathematics by simply exchanging the positions of Earth and the sun, making the sun the centerpiece. But Digges extended the Copernican scheme to include the idea that the universe is infinite. Once Digges had made this extension, he saw the problem that would puzzle Olbers some 250 years later. Digges, however, did not analyze the problem as carefully as Olbers would, and Digges concluded that the reason the nighttime sky is not bright was simply that the more distant stars were too dim to be seen on Earth—an answer similar to the one we're most familiar with, but not the right answer.

Giordano Bruno, another supporter and contemporary of

Digges, agreed with Digges that the universe was infinite. This radical idea, as Bruno pointed out, made meaningless the whole notion of some point being the center of the universe—most especially Earth. How could something of infinite extent have a center? Bruno was burned at the stake in 1600 for expounding this and other heretical notions.

In 1610 Johannes Kepler, the father of modern mathematical astronomy, wrote: "If this is true [that the universe is infinite and has a uniform distribution of stars] and if they are suns having the same nature as our Sun, why do not these suns collectively outdistance our Sun in brilliance? Why do they all together transmit so dim a light to the most accessible places?" Kepler's conclusion was that the universe could not be infinite. He felt so strongly on this point that he wrote to Galileo: "You do not hesitate to declare that there are visible over 10,000 stars. The more there are, and the more crowded they are, the stronger becomes my argument against the infinity of the universe."

At the time there seemed to be only two possible conclusions: Either there was a cosmic edge beyond which there were no stars (suns) and therefore a dark night sky, or the universe was infinite with a blazing sky both day and night. Given these two alternatives, the correct answer seemed obvious: Newton's belief that the universe is eternal and infinite with a uniform distribution of stars must be wrong because with Olbers' flawless argument, there is no escaping a lighted sky both day and night in Newton's version of the universe.

About one hundred twenty years after Bruno's death, Edmund Halley, after whom Halley's comet is named, presented a scientific paper to the Royal Society of London in which he pointed out the problem of the dark nighttime sky. Isaac Newton, who was in charge of the meeting, agreed that Halley's logic was sound and that there was a genuine puzzle. What probably puzzled the participants at the meeting even more than Halley's discussion was that the problem had never occurred to the genius Newton. Newton was, after all, the authority on the subject of optics, the science of light; and it was incredible that he should have overlooked so observable a problem.

By the nineteenth century some persons other than scientists had become interested in Olbers' paradox. Edgar Allan Poe was one of them. In "Eureka: A Prose Poem" he proposed that as we look out into space, we look back in time and eventually see the nothingness that existed before the birth of the universe—a suggestion completely at odds with Newton's universe, infinite in space and time.

It is not unusual in science for an important clue to a puzzle's solution to be already at hand but not recognized at the time. Such was the case with Olbers' paradox. In 1675, long before Olbers' birth, the Danish astronomer Ole Roemer had provided an important key to the solution of the paradox, although this was not the subject of his work and no one saw the connection at the time, or even later. Through some clever observations of the moons of the planet Jupiter, he proved that light travels with finite, not infinite, speed, as many of his time believed. In retrospect, given this observation of Roemer's, it is perhaps surprising that the resolution of Olbers' paradox had to await the knowledge and technology of the twentieth century. Roemer's observation that light travels with finite speed is the key to unraveling the paradox. And this key, combined with the observed fact of the dark nighttime sky, leads almost directly to Poe's anachronistic suggestion that the universe had a beginning. We shall say much more about all this in Chapter 9.

No problem has perplexed man more throughout the ages

than the origin, structure, and evolution of the universe. Legends and folktales from different cultures in all parts of the world suggest fanciful answers. The problem is at the heart of much religious doctrine and ceremony; every religion has a genesis story. And philosophical speculation and argument today continue to revolve around the whole question of creation and evolution, how the universe began—if in fact it had a beginning—what it's made of, and how it works. Even humor embraces the subject. An amusing English music hall verse says,

> *There are holes in the sky*
> *Where the rain gets in,*
> *But the holes are small;*
> *That's why rain is thin.*

The method of reasoning in the verse is not too far removed from the method of modern science. The verse provides an explanation of why rain is thin, and the argument reversed— noticing first that rain *is* thin—suggests not only that there are holes in the sky but that they must be small.

It is not rain, however, but the light that so perplexed Olbers that provides us with our best understanding of the structure and nature of the universe. But this light reaches well beyond the light that the human eye can see. Just as there are high-frequency sound waves that dogs can hear but human ears cannot, there are also light waves both above and below the frequencies that the human eye can detect. Just knowing this helps us set aside some of the "obvious" answers we've accepted to questions about the universe and, thinking more like scientists, to consider answers that may appear illogical.

In the past few decades a whole array of new tools has allowed us to peer into the universe and "see" things the eye has never seen. These tools help us resolve problems like Olbers' paradox, and at the same time uncover new problems and mysteries that no one had ever suspected before. The universe visible to the naked eye—or even the eye helped by the most powerful telescope—only hints in the faintest way at the richness and variety of the unseen and unseeable universe. This universe and the instruments that have revealed it are the subject of this book.

2

Visible and Invisible Light

Until just a few decades ago, almost all we knew about the universe had been gleaned from observing the light of stars. Many of them are so far away that their light has traveled thousands and even millions of years to reach us. The first telescopes, during the time of Galileo, revealed that some of the points of light in the night skies were not points at all, but were in fact small balls of light. We know now that these balls are the planets—Mars, Venus, Jupiter, and so on—which, like Earth, endlessly circle the sun. But even with later, more powerful telescopes, other points of light remained just that—points of light—simply because they were too far away to appear as anything else. These more distant sources of light, the stars, are in many ways very much like our own sun.

Unlike the planets, whose presence is revealed by light reflected from the sun, the stars generate their own light from intense nuclear furnaces at their cores. Although we cannot study the surface features of stars the way we can those of the moon and the planets, we can learn a great deal about them by studying the kinds of light they generate. In fact, what we have learned about the composition, birth, life, and death of stars just from examining their light is amazing.

To understand how we have learned so much about the universe by sifting starlight, we need to think about the nature of light. Most of us already know that when sunlight passes through a prism, the result is a familiar "rainbow" of colors. As we shall see in more detail later, every particular color has a particular vibration rate, or *frequency.* For now we can say that as we move through the *spectrum* of colors from red through orange and yellow, green to violet, we move from lower to higher frequencies.

Colors, however, make up only a very small part of the light spectrum. Light in the natural world is not restricted to a certain set of frequencies, and we cannot *see* all frequencies because our eyes respond to only a limited range of them; but as we shall learn, it's the frequencies we cannot see that enable us to look at things that are invisible to our eyes.

As early as 1800, scientists had noticed that a thermometer held just beyond the red end of the solar spectrum—a region where nothing whatever is visible to the eye—showed a temperature rise. Some invisible radiation seemed to be heating the thermometer. Today we call this *infrared* radiation, and we often place electric bulbs that produce prolific infrared radiation in bathrooms for a quick and ready source of heat. As further studies were to show, about 60 percent of the total energy radiated from the sun is infrared radiation.

At the other end of the solar spectrum—just beyond the violet end, where again nothing is visible to the eye—scientists found something else strange. When silver salts, commonly used to make photographic paper sensitive to light, were exposed to this part of the spectrum, they darkened much faster than they did in normal sunlight. Again there seemed to be some mysterious radiation invisible to the eye. Today we call this *ultraviolet* radiation, because it is beyond the violet end of the spectrum. Most of us have experienced this radiation as sunburn, sometimes painful and serious. Fortunately, Earth's atmosphere filters out most of the deadly ultraviolet radiation from the sun. See Figure 1.

Before the beginning of the nineteenth century, electricity and magnetism were thought to be two different phenomena,

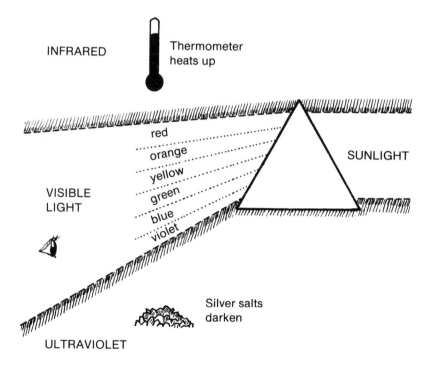

fig. 1

and neither one was thought of as light. Scientists produced sparks in their laboratories by rubbing various materials with silk handkerchiefs, and they also experimented with bits of iron clinging to magnets. Then it was discovered that electric currents in wires produce magnetic fields, and that moving magnets produce electric currents in wires. James Clerk Maxwell, a mathematician from Scotland, was aware of the demonstrated connection between electricity and magnetism. Near the middle of the nineteenth century, he showed that they are really two sides of the same coin.

One of the remarkable offspring of this marriage between electricity and magnetism was the prediction that there should be some sort of wave consisting of electric and magnetic fields that spread through space—an *electromagnetic* wave. The theory predicted at precisely what speed these electromagnetic waves should move; and the curious thing was that the predicted speed was exactly the speed of light, which had been measured many years before. Either there was a most extraordinary coincidence in nature, or light was in fact an electromagnetic wave.

Today we know that visible light is just one form of electromagnetic radiation, and radio waves are another. What separates visible light waves from radio waves is simply a matter of frequency; light waves are at high frequencies that our eyes can see, whereas radio waves are at frequencies too low for our eyes to detect.

Scientists have identified and studied a whole spectrum of electromagnetic radiation. Figure 2 shows the various parts of this spectrum. Besides visible light waves we have infrared radiation just below the frequencies our eyes can see. At still lower frequencies we have the microwave region, where radar and microwave ovens operate, and below this the radio region.

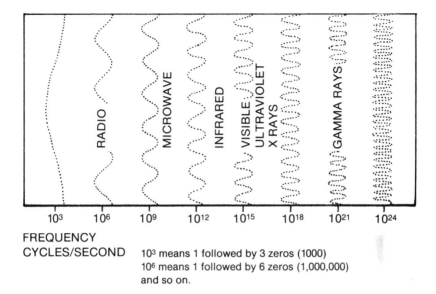

FREQUENCY
CYCLES/SECOND   10³ means 1 followed by 3 zeros (1000)
                 10⁶ means 1 followed by 6 zeros (1,000,000)
                 and so on.

fig. 2

Just above the visible part of the spectrum we have the ultravio-let region, and above this are X rays, used routinely to photo-graph broken bones. At even higher frequencies we have gamma rays, which, as we shall see, have revealed many things about the universe.

Overall, we see that the visible part of the spectrum is just a sliver of the total electromagnetic spectrum. This suggests that what we learned about the universe by observing only the visible parts has been just a sliver of what was to be learned as scientists discovered how to make observations outside the visible region.

All of the parts, both visible and invisible, are thought of today as light; and scientists speak of "looking at" invisible things they "see" with invisible light in the same way that other people look at objects in the visible universe. From now on, we, too, shall think of both visible and invisible radiation as light.

Now that we know something of how visible light fits into the electromagnetic spectrum, let's backtrack to the year 1814, when a German optician, Joseph von Fraunhofer, discovered something strange and remarkable. Fraunhofer found that when he let a beam of sunlight pass through a prism and then greatly magnified the rainbow that emerged from the opposite side of the prism, he obtained the usual spectrum of colors ranging from red to violet. But interspersed throughout the spectrum were hundreds of black lines, as shown in Figure 3. For some reason, sunlight did not produce a continuous spectrum of colors. Instead, it created a spectrum from which some shades or blends of colors were missing, leaving in their place the black lines. He also discovered that the same pattern of lines existed

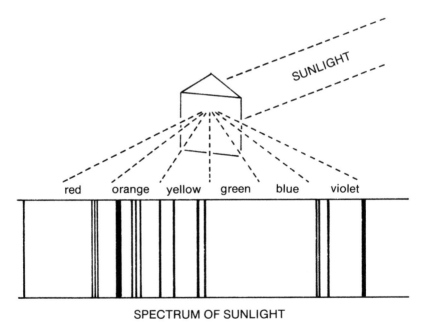

SPECTRUM OF SUNLIGHT

fig. 3

in the sunlight reflected from the planets and the moon, and in the light from some of the stars, but not all. Other sources of light did not produce this same pattern, although some sources had their own distinctive pattern of lines. It was as though sunlight could be "fingerprinted" by its unique series of black lines.

As Fraunhofer continued his studies, he eventually identified more than six hundred of the strange dark lines in the spectrum of the sun. He labeled the most prominent lines with the letters A, B, C, and so on—a system that holds to this day. Fraunhofer had no explanation for his discovery, but as we shall see, his observation was crucial to our understanding of the composition of stars.

While Fraunhofer was doing his experiments, other scientists studied the spectra of various kinds of materials by heating them to temperatures that made them glow—substances such as potassium, sodium, and chromium. The spectrum of sodium contained two dark lines that coincided exactly with two lines Fraunhofer had labeled D1 and D2 in his studies of the sun. Could this mean that the sun contained the element sodium?

As scientists studied the spectral lines of more and more substances, they realized that many of the lines observed in the spectrum of the sun were identical with lines produced by such earthly elements as iron, carbon, and hydrogen. There seemed to be growing evidence that many of the elements found on Earth were also in the sun. But no one was really sure because no one had any real understanding of just where the spectral lines came from.

There were also lines in the solar spectrum that did not correspond to any lines observed on Earth. One of the most prominent sets of such lines was observed during an eclipse of the sun in 1868. The mystery substance believed to be responsible for the lines was called *helium*, a Greek word for sun. It was not until some thirty years later that helium was found on Earth.

At about the same time Fraunhofer and other observers were studying the dark lines in various spectra, other scientists noticed that some sources of light yielded a different kind of spectrum; instead of dark lines, there were *bright* lines superimposed on the uniform background spectrum. This discovery was also to prove crucial to the future development of astronomy. In Chapter 4 we shall say more about these dark and bright lines. But first we must learn something about the relationship between light and temperature, and the so-called blackbody problem.

3

The Ultraviolet Catastrophe

The blackbody problem bothered scientists for a good part of the nineteenth century and continued to bother them well into our own century. What is a blackbody and why does it present a problem? A blackbody is any substance that absorbs all of the light, both visible and invisible, that falls upon it. This, of course, includes all colors. Most bodies that we might think of as black are not blackbodies in the scientific sense, because almost all substances reflect some light, however little. If a black cat were truly black, we would not be able to see it at all, except as a silhouette against some bright background, because no light would be reflected from it into our eyes. Ordinary soot comes closer to being a blackbody. But a perfect blackbody exists only in theory, as something that physicists study and discuss.

A blackbody is black only when it is relatively cool. Surprisingly enough, a star—our own brilliant sun, for example—is a fairly good representation of a blackbody. How can this be? Well, let's suppose that we heat a body, soot or a piece of iron perhaps, to the point that it glows. We know from experience that when we heat such a body to higher and higher temperatures, its glow becomes brighter and the color changes. First we see a dull red; then the red turns to orange, then to yellow, then to blue; finally we say the object is white hot. Thus, just as a blackbody absorbs light of all colors when it is cool, it emits light of all colors when it is hot.

Furthermore, even though we see only a predominant color at each stage, the body is still radiating, to a lesser degree, at all colors of the rainbow and also at all invisible frequencies both below and above the color band. If we suppose, for example, that our piece of soot has a temperature of just one degree, which is far below the visible range, it still radiates a very tiny bit of every color, even though the amount is so small that we cannot see it.

While we are gaining a sense of light as being both visible and invisible, we need also to understand some facts about heat. We tend to think of heat in terms of the warmth our bodies feel. But the infrared heat that we feel is only a part of the heat spectrum. We know that on a cloudy day at the beach, or even on a cold, snow-covered ski slope, we may experience sunburn from ultraviolet rays that penetrate the clouds and reflect from water or snow. We know that X rays can cause dangerous burns, as can radiation from uranium and other radioactive elements. So heat is not necessarily something we can feel. We should think of it more as a form of energy.

Near the end of the last century, scientists measured very carefully how the color of a blackbody changes with temperature. They found that for any particular temperature, the radiated light increased with frequency until it reached a peak at a particular color—or frequency—and then decreased again for even higher frequencies. In other words, at any particular temperature we *see* the particular color that represents the frequency that peaks at that temperature. If we look at the curve labeled 6,000 degrees in Figure 1, for example, we see how a blackbody heated to 6,000 degrees radiates light at different frequencies. The frequency at which this particular curve peaks is that of the color yellow, as the figure shows.

What happens now if we add more heat to the body to increase its temperature? Scientists found that the amount of light radiated at all frequencies increased, as the figure shows. The curve labeled 12,000 degrees is at every frequency above the curves labeled 6,000 degrees and 3,000 degrees. That is, at any

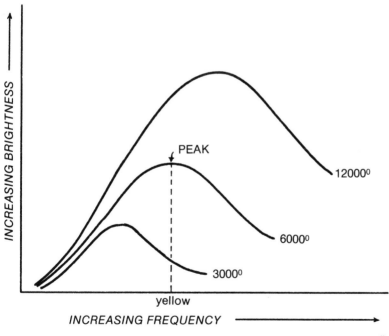

fig. 1

frequency we might choose, the radiated light is always brighter at 12,000 degrees than it is at any lower temperature.

Scientists also found that as they increased the temperature of a blackbody, its peak moved to higher and higher frequencies—toward the blue-violet part of the spectrum, in the visible band. In the figure, we see that the peak for a blackbody at 12,000 degrees is at a higher frequency than the peak frequency for a blackbody at 3,000 degrees.

The final important fact the scientists found was that the total amount of energy radiated by a blackbody increased dramatically with temperature; each time the temperature of a blackbody doubled, its total energy output increased sixteen times.

The astronomers of the day quickly understood that these measurements were important for them. From the color of a star they could estimate its surface temperature; and once they knew its temperature, they could estimate the amount of energy the star radiated.

This information immediately raised a big problem. It was obvious from the observations that a typical star was radiating huge amounts of energy every second. But where could this energy come from? It couldn't be from the usual sources of energy such as wood or coal, because the star would soon exhaust such an energy supply. Only some new energy source could explain it. Today, of course, we know that the stars are fired by the equivalent of thousands of nuclear bombs exploding continually in their dense, hot interiors. But we are getting ahead of our story.

By the end of the nineteenth century, the radiation characteristics of blackbodies were well understood. What was not understood at all was *why* blackbodies radiated the way they did—why the peak frequencies increased with temperature, for example. Some of the best scientific theorists of the time attacked the problem. Most theories were based on the idea that energy should be radiated equally at all frequencies. This idea explained the increase of energy radiated with increasing frequency for a particular temperature. But it had one flaw—a fatal flaw—the so-called ultraviolet catastrophe.

To understand the ultraviolet catastrophe, let's imagine a special kind of piano. Instead of producing sound at a particular frequency when a certain key is struck, this piano produces a light signal with a frequency that depends on the key that is struck. The keys on the left, or bass, side of the keyboard that normally generate low-frequency notes now generate low-frequency light signals, and those at the right end of the keyboard generate high-frequency light signals from a bulb attached to the piano.

If we ran a finger from left to right on this keyboard, it would generate the whole spectrum of colors, from red on the low-frequency end to violet on the high-frequency end. We would see the same spectrum of light that we see when we view sunlight passed through a prism or when we see a rainbow.

Now we want to make one other modification to our light piano. Unlike a normal piano, which can play only a lowest note and a highest note and all the notes in between, our light piano has keys that extend on the left all the way down to the very lowest frequency possible, zero cycles per second. And on the right it has keys all the way out to the highest frequency possible—an infinite number of cycles per second. The reason for this is that, as we have seen, light in the natural world is not restricted to a certain set of frequencies. Although we can see only a limited range of frequencies, frequencies below and above this range are as real and present as the color frequencies and are emitted right along with them.

Now that we have a piano that generates light over an infinite range of frequencies, we can see how the ultraviolet catastrophe comes about. Suppose we touch some key at random on our light piano. There will always be more notes to the right of this key than to the left. This is so because the lowest note we can have on our piano is zero frequency, whereas the highest note has infinite frequency. (This same thing is true of positive numbers. If we choose any number at random—say 474,987,590,827—there will be only 474,987,590,826 numbers smaller, but an infinite number of numbers larger than the one we chose.) So if we press all of the keys above any key we choose at random, all of those keys will generate an infinite amount of energy because there are always an infinite number of keys beyond the randomly chosen key.

What has all this to do with the ultraviolet catastrophe? Well, ultraviolet light is just beyond the highest frequency that the eye can see. But there are always an infinite number of frequencies higher than any we can observe as visible light. As we said earlier, the predominant theory of the time assumed that all frequencies are generated with equal probability. Carried to its ultimate conclusion, this theory would say that all this invisible light at all of these frequencies, infinite in number, would pile up to produce infinite energy in the universe, since light is a form of energy. This infinite energy would heat all substances in the universe to infinite temperature—obviously an unacceptable catastrophe.

The situation is somewhat like Olbers' paradox. Olbers saw that if the prevailing light theories of his time were true, the whole universe should be infinitely bright. Similarly, the theories believed to relate energy and temperature would result in a universe that was infinitely hot. What we need, instead of a theory based on the idea that all keys of our light piano are equally likely to be pressed, is some theory in which the keys above a certain note are less likely to be pressed than those below this note.

In 1899, Max Karl Ludwig Planck tackled the problem. As a student, Planck had talked with his teacher about his wish to become a physicist. His teacher told him that physics was dead; everything had been discovered and there was no future in physics. He advised Planck instead to become a concert pianist—and he was not referring to our light piano! Fortunately for physics, Planck did not take the advice but became one of the most distinguished German physicists of modern times.

Planck was well aware of the dilemmas posed by the prevailing theory, even though he was also convinced that it was mathematically correct. There was, he decided, only one possible alternative: The assumption that all energy frequencies were generated with equal probability must be wrong.

In his search for a new theory, Planck faced the two undeniable facts that we have just discussed: First, the amount of radiated energy increases with frequency until it reaches peak frequency, then decreases with frequencies beyond this peak. Second, there is an infinity of frequencies above any particular frequency.

At this point Planck took, for the times, a daring step. He assumed that the radiated energy did not flow smoothly and continuously from a blackbody. This was a radical idea because physicists had always assumed that nature's processes were smooth and continuous; the planets do not fitfully start and stop as they move around the sun; water is a continuous, uniformly dense substance.

Planck imagined that the energy radiated from a blackbody consisted of minute buckets of energy—*quanta*, he called

Fortunately for science, Max Planck chose to become a physicist instead of a concert pianist.

them—and that the amount of energy in each bucket was directly proportional to the frequency of the light associated with that bucket. That is, a bucket of red light contains less energy than a bucket of blue light because red corresponds to a lower radiation frequency than that of blue.

Let's see how this idea explains the observed blackbody radiation curve. A bucket of light energy corresponding to the color red would contain about half as much energy as a bucket corresponding to the color violet because violet has a frequency about two times that of red. In other words, the higher the frequency the greater the amount of radiated energy—up to a peak for each particular frequency. But why is there then a *drop* in radiated energy after the peak frequency is reached?

The explanation is not difficult. Since a violet bucket contains twice as much energy as a red bucket, it will take the violet bucket longer to fill—or to *absorb* this larger amount of energy—before it can emit its energy. The situation is somewhat like a crowd of people leaving a concert and looking for taxis with different carrying capacities. Under such circumstances, cab drivers often will not leave until their taxis are filled. This means that the larger taxis will take longer to fill; but when they do leave, they will be carrying more people.

This taking longer to fill explains why energy emission decreases with increasing frequency above the peak frequency. That is, it takes longer to fill a violet bucket than to fill a red one. Or in terms of our piano analogy, the higher we go up the scale, the less likely a key is to be pressed—just what we were looking for to explain the drop-off in radiated energy above the peak frequency. So we see that *below* the peak frequency, the amount of radiated energy increases with frequency; but *above* the peak frequency, the decreasing likelihood of radiation starts to dominate.

The other fact to explain is that the peak frequency increases as the temperature of the blackbody increases. Here we can return to our taxi analogy. Consider two concerts where the attendance at one is moderate, and at the other, standing room only. The concert hall, although very large, is well designed, with many interior corridors and exits, so the time it takes to empty the hall does not depend on how many people are inside. In the moderate-attendance case, all cabs of all sizes will fill more slowly than the same set of cabs for the standing-room-only case, simply because the people straggle out a few at a time and so there are fewer people looking for cabs at the smaller concert. The particular cab size for which the rate of filling is just balanced by the rate of cabs departing depends on the initial crowd size. Or put a little differently, the balance-point cab size will increase as the size of the crowd increases. This balance point corresponds to the peak frequency on our radiation curve; the crowd size corresponds to the temperature. Thus the peak frequency increases with temperature.

Of course, what we have been describing in words, Planck worked out in precise mathematical fashion, producing an equation that predicted the observed temperature-radiation variation with convincing accuracy. The problem was that nobody really believed in Planck's buckets of radiation, the quanta. Not even Planck himself.

But as time was to show, Planck's radical idea was a watershed in the history of physics. The curve, which was very familiar to scientists, became known as the Planck Radiation Curve. Today most physicists think of all the physics before Planck's radiation theory as belonging to *classical* physics, whereas Planck's quanta ushered in the age of *modern* physics. Planck's teacher had been right; there was no future in classical physics. But Planck himself had unwittingly ushered in a whole new physics with a bright and exciting future.

And now that we know something about the relationship between color and energy and temperature and heat, we're ready to go back to the story of Fraunhofer's strange dark lines and see how they turned out to be related to Planck's buckets of light in a way that no classical physicist could ever have imagined.

4

Pinchfuls of Starlight

During the end of the nineteenth century and into the first part of the twentieth century, scientists accumulated a considerable body of observations related to the spectra of various substances as well as the spectra of many astronomical bodies. Most scientists were convinced that these spectra revealed a good deal about the constitution of stars. Astronomers had long used colors of stars to estimate their temperatures, just as blacksmiths judge the temperature of a hot metal from its color. By the time of Planck's studies of the variation in color of a substance with temperature, the colors of some four thousand stars had been studied and classified.

There seemed to be three main types of stars: the white-blue stars, the yellow stars, and the red stars. Presumably the white-blue stars were the hottest, followed by the yellow stars, and coolest, the red stars. There was also a relatively small group of red stars with unexpected dark lines. And the best-known star of all, our sun, clearly showed during solar eclipses that, in addition to Fraunhofer's dark lines, there were bright lines in its outer atmosphere, the corona.

Scientists had also made other significant observations. Experiments had shown that although our eyes see only the predominant color, hot glowing objects actually emit a continuous rainbow of colors all at the same time. The situation is somewhat like an orchestra in which all the instruments are playing together but the trumpets are blaring so loudly that we hear only the trumpets.

Scientists had further observed that when they viewed a glowing object producing a continuous spectrum through some cooler gas—the atmosphere, for example—dark lines appeared. And strangely enough, the dark lines they saw depended on the kind of gas. Viewing a glowing object through hydrogen gas produced a different set of dark lines than viewing the same object through oxygen. Finally, scientists noted that if they looked through a cooler gas from an angle, so as to avoid looking directly at the glowing object, then where the *dark* lines had been, there were now, at exactly the same positions, *bright* lines.

It appeared that somehow the atoms in the gas absorbed the continuous light passing through them at very specific frequencies, producing the dark lines in the otherwise continuous spectrum of light. But when the same object was viewed at an angle, the dark lines became bright lines. This suggested that the atoms that were absorbing certain frequencies of the radiation coming from the direction of the glowing source were radiating that light at the same frequencies. But this radiation was not just in the direction of the light coming in from the source; instead, it shone uniformly in all directions, as shown in Figure 1.

The situation is something like water passing through a garden hose into a sprinkler head that redirects the water uniformly in all directions. The water passing through the hose represents

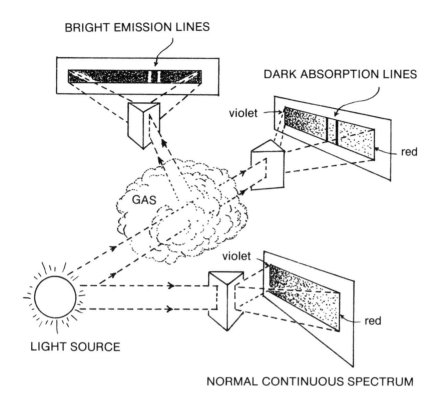

DARK ABSORPTION LINES

violet

red

GAS

violet

red

LIGHT SOURCE

NORMAL CONTINUOUS SPECTRUM

fig. 1

the glowing light source at a particular frequency. Without the sprinkler head, when we look directly at the stream flowing from the hose, we see a strong rush of water—the undiminished light at a particular frequency. Then, if we add a sprinkler head—which corresponds to putting a cool gas in front of the light source—we see a reduction in the flow of water; that is, there's an *absorption line.* But when we look in other directions, we see water spraying where we had not seen it before; that is, we see *emission lines,* because the sprinkler—the atoms in the cool gas—has redirected the water along paths in which it had not previously flowed.

Observations of these kinds gave some hints concerning the

peculiar red stars with the unusual dark absorption lines. Apparently they were produced by some cooler gas surrounding the red star generating the light. On the other hand, the bright emission lines from the solar corona must come about because we are not looking directly at the sun, but into the gas that makes up the corona surrounding the sun. But such observations raised more questions than they answered, and the mysterious dark and bright lines observed by Fraunhofer and others continued to baffle scientists.

The unraveling of the mystery came in a roundabout way. In 1911 a young Danish physicist, Niels Bohr, arrived at J. J. Thomson's Cavindish Laboratory in England. Thomson, the discoverer of the electron, was one of the world's most famous physicists. Bohr counted himself fortunate to have been invited to work in Thomson's laboratory.

Thomson's work, and that of others, suggested that an atom consisted of some kind of mixture of positive and negative electrical charges. Thomson proposed that the atom was something like a raisin pudding, with negative electrons sprinkled like so many raisins throughout a smeared-out volume of smooth, positive electrical charge, as shown in Figure 2.

smeared-out positive charge

electron

fig. 2

ATOM

Niels Bohr
said the atom
was like a small
solar system.

Many scientists, including Bohr, tried to use Thomson's model of the atom to calculate the light emission that one would expect from such an atom. But it soon became clear to Bohr and others that no amount of calculation would reconcile Thomson's atom with the absorption and emission lines that by this time were well known.

Bohr kept coming back to Planck's assumption that light was emitted—and presumably therefore also absorbed—in discrete buckets of energy—the quanta. But as we have said, Planck himself was not pleased with this idea, and Thomson even less so. Bohr finally left Thomson's laboratory because he, Bohr, did not believe in the raisin-pudding atom. He went to the University of Manchester to work in Ernest Rutherford's laboratory, and this move turned out to be one of the most fortunate incidents in the history of science.

Rutherford, an immensely talented experimental physicist, had discovered that the atom was not at all what Thomson had proposed. Instead of having electrons scattered throughout a smeared-out positive electrical charge, the atom had a dense central core of positive charge surrounded by a sea of electrons. Rutherford's discovery, along with Planck's quanta, were the two key ingredients that led Bohr to his revolutionary model of the atom.

Bohr realized that Rutherford's atom could not be understood within the laws of electricity and magnetism known at that time. The problem was that the sea of negative electrons surrounding the atom's central core, the *nucleus,* would crash into the nucleus within less than a millionth of a second because of the strong electrical attraction between the negative electrons and the positive electrical charge of the nucleus. It was at this point that Bohr used Planck's quanta of light to help solve the problem.

Let's consider a very simple atom, the hydrogen atom, to see what Bohr proposed. The hydrogen atom has just one electron, whose negative charge is balanced by an equal and opposite positive charge at the nucleus of the atom. Bohr said that this single electron circled the nucleus much as Earth circles the sun. As we have said, according to the laws of electricity and magnetism accepted at the time, this single electron should almost instantaneously crash into the nucleus.

But Bohr made a startling suggestion. He said the electron could circle continuously around the nucleus without falling inward. He said further that when the electron did move inward, it moved essentially instantaneously to a new orbit closer to the nucleus, as Figure 3 shows, and not all the way into the nucleus. Later on, the electron might move into an even closer orbit, as the figure also shows. Furthermore, according to Bohr, the electron could not move into just any orbit, but must move into only certain orbits, such as those labeled 1, 2, and 3 in the figure.

An electron could also move from an inner to an outer orbit, as the figure shows. But what makes an electron jump to an outer orbit? According to Bohr, this happens when the atom absorbs light energy of just the right amount—which, as we recall from

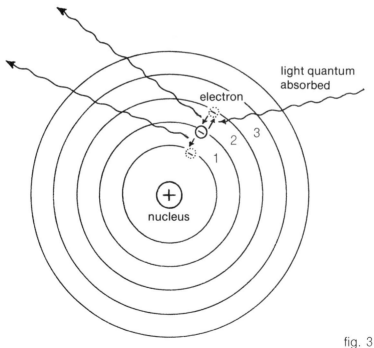

fig. 3

Planck's theory, means that the light must be at a particular frequency.

The situation is a little like carrying a bucket of sand up a flight of stairs. It takes a certain amount of energy to lift the bucket from one step to the next. If we don't have that much energy, we can't get the bucket to the next step; we must leave the bucket where it is. There is no such thing as lifting the bucket up just half a step; it's the whole step or nothing. And so it is with the electron. It can't move just part way to another orbit, but must move outward all the way to the next allowable orbit.

Now we are beginning to see how an atom absorbs light energy. When light of just the right energy—or frequency—needed to move an electron to an allowed outer orbit strikes the atom, the atom absorbs the energy. This causes an electron to jump to an outer orbit. Sometimes there may be just the right amount of energy to move an electron from, say orbit 1 to orbit 3. That would be like lifting a bucket of sand up two steps at a time instead of just one.

We have mentioned just three allowed orbits, but in fact there may be any number, as the figure shows. Which of these orbits an electron moves to depends simply on the amount of energy absorbed by the atom; the more energy it absorbs, the farther out the orbit to which the electron moves.

These observations put us in a position to understand how the dark lines in spectra form. When a continuous spectrum of light passes through a cool gas, such as Earth's atmosphere, some of the light energy is absorbed by atoms of the gas whose electrons move into higher orbits. But only the light energy at the frequencies that allow the electron to jump in the atom is absorbed. This is why the absorption is very specific with regard to frequency, and why the patterns of dark lines are very consistent. Light energy corresponding to other frequencies is not absorbed because there are no corresponding energy levels in the atoms that make up the gas.

We can turn our observations around now to explain the bright emission lines in spectra. When an electron jumps to a *lower* orbit, it *emits* a specific amount of energy. For example, if the electron in Figure 3 jumps from orbit 2 to orbit 1, it emits exactly the same amount of energy that it took to move the electron initially from orbit 1 to 2. And since energy and the frequency of the radiation are directly related, all of the energy is emitted at a specific frequency, giving rise to a particular spectral emission line.

We can see now that Bohr's theory also explains where Planck's buckets of energy come from. In fact, Bohr's theory worked so well that most scientists, even those who were skeptical of Planck's theory, began to believe that light energy did indeed travel in discrete or quantized chunks.

One of the believers was a young English scientist, Cecilia Payne. She had heard both Bohr and Rutherford discuss their work while she was a student in England. In 1923, at the age of twenty-three, she arrived in Boston to do graduate work at the Harvard College Observatory. This was the repository of a collection of more than a quarter million slides of star spectra made during the early 1920s by an outstanding astronomy scholar, Annie Jump Cannon. So great was Dr. Cannon's devotion to this project that it was said she could identify, almost immediately, any particular star simply by looking at its spectra, just as we recognize dozens of friends and acquaintances by their faces.

Payne immediately realized how Bohr's theory of atomic absorption and emission of light could be used to interpret the

Cecilia Payne realized she could use the Bohr atom to explain the bright and dark lines in the spectra of stars.

Annie Jump Cannon made more than a quarter of a million slides of star spectra.

maze of slides. After several years of study, she was able to identify many elements from the "pinchfuls" of starlight collected by Cannon.

One of Payne's most important discoveries had to do with the element calcium—the main element found in bones and shells. When an electron in the calcium atom jumps from the next to the lowest orbit, orbit 2, to the lowest orbit, orbit 1, in the quantum ladder, it emits light in the violet end of the spectrum. Payne studied this same line over and over in many different stars and discovered something peculiar. In the brightest, hottest stars—the white-blue stars—the line was rather dim; but as she moved toward the cooler stars—the red stars—the line became brighter.

By this time Bohr's theory had been developed to the point that Payne was able to propose an explanation for this peculiar result. She reasoned that for the calcium to emit light at the particular violet line she was studying, it must first have absorbed just the right amount of energy to jump from orbit 1 to orbit 2. In the cool red stars, most of the light energy is at low frequencies corresponding to jumps in the electrons of the calcium atom between orbits 1 and 2. The red stars, she reasoned, are not energetic enough to jump the electrons into higher orbits. So this particular violet line is quite strong in cool stars because there is a lot of electron movement back and forth between the first two orbits of the calcium atom.

In hotter stars there may be just as many calcium atoms, but the energy in these stars is enough to allow the electrons to jump back and forth between many different orbits; so now the emitted radiation energy is not concentrated in just the violet line, but is spread over a wide range of frequencies corresponding to the many allowed jumps. In this way Payne was able to explain why the violet line is stronger in cool stars than in hot stars. This work was the subject of her dissertation for her Ph.D. degree—a dissertation many astronomers believe is the best thesis ever written in astronomy.

In later years Dr. Payne continued her study of the lines in the stellar spectra of many different kinds of elements. In this way, using Bohr's theory, she was able to produce a remarkably consistent picture of the composition of stars and how their spectra are related to stellar temperatures. She was able to show that, for the most part, all stars are made of the same kind of stuff, and that differences in the spectra from star to star are more a matter of differences in temperature than anything else.

One of her most significant conclusions was that typical stars have large abundances of the two lightest elements, hydrogen and helium, which we put into balloons to make them float in air. The other, heavier elements were found in about the same proportions as they are found here on Earth.

Next we shall learn how a whole new school of astronomy, the radio astronomers, discovered that not only are stars packed with hydrogen, but that, in fact, hydrogen fills most of the space between stars. Radio astronomers, as their name implies, use only the very low, invisible frequencies at the radio end of the electromagnetic spectrum to make their observations.

5

Scruff, Chad, and LGMs

By 1931 radio telephones were common, but there were some problems. One had to do with the crackling noise on radio-telephone circuits during thunderstorms. A young engineer from the Bell Telephone Laboratories, Karl Jansky, was sent out to investigate the problem and see if he could develop some scheme to get rid of the crackling, or at least reduce it.

To start his investigation, Jansky set up an antenna and receiver in a potato field near his laboratory in New Jersey. Much to his surprise, he found that not all of the radio noise came from thunderstorms; some of it came from the direction of the Milky Way galaxy. Jansky's discovery created considerable excitement among astronomers and other scientists. The popular press also showed interest; the *New York Times* featured Jansky's work on page one.

But in spite of the stir created by the discovery, the work was dropped. The world was in the midst of the Great Depression. Money for research was in short supply, and there was talk of

Karl Jansky discovered radio noise coming from the direction of the Milky Way.

closing Jansky's laboratory. Then, in a few short years, the world became embroiled in World War II. Like many other scientists and engineers, Jansky redirected his work toward the war effort.

By the time the war was over, Jansky's health had failed, and he did not live to see the upheaval that radio astronomy spawned in our understanding of the universe. Ironically, the development of radar during World War II led to early important discoveries in this new branch of astronomy. We shall say more about this later.

The work started by Jansky was carried on during the depression almost single-handedly by Grote Reber, a talented, irascible American radio ham who built the first radio telescope, as we call it now, in his backyard in Wheaton, Illinois. The antenna of his radio telescope had the familiar dish shape we often see in backyards today pointed at a communications satellite that broadcasts television signals.

Reber described the reaction of curious passersby to his "peculiar contraption": "Cars frequently would stop, people would get out, walk around . . . and take pictures. Some even had the fortitude to ring the doorbell and inquire about the purpose of the contraption. . . . At one time, I considered placing a jukebox out in front with a sign 'Drop Quarter in Slot and Find Out What This Is All About.' "

Using his contraption, Reber systematically charted the radio signals from the Milky Way to provide a contour map that showed how the radio signals differed in strength from one part of the Milky Way to the next. When he first presented his work to the astronomical community, they were skeptical and refused to publish his results. Fortunately, however, the editor of the *Astronomical Journal* saw the importance of his work and eventually published it.

Grote Reber
built the first
radio telescope.

Reber's association with the established scientific community, especially the astronomers, was never smooth. On one occasion, when Reber wished to publish a new finding, the editor of the *Astronomical Journal* sent out a group of reporters on a Monday morning to find out what was going on. Reber refused to move his antenna to demonstrate his findings because his mother was using it to anchor one end of her clothesline. Even today Reber's relationship with mainstream astronomers is abrasive.

When we read accounts of new scientific discoveries, we often get the feeling that everything goes smoothly, according to plan. We think that one experiment leads logically to the next and culminates in the expected result. This feeling is due largely to the way scientists publish the results of their work. In learned scientific journals they lay out the various parts of the experiment in a very logical and orderly manner. They give the result of each intermediate step and end with their conclusions. So it always looks very straightforward and logically consistent. But the truth is that almost no experiment ever goes this way—especially if it yields an important result. And sometimes some of the most important results are unexpected results of fortuitous accidents.

One of the important discoveries in radio astronomy occurred accidentally during World War II. A civilian working for the British army set up a system to detect German jamming of the British radar network. Radar works by transmitting a series of short radio pulses, which, if they hit an object—such as an enemy airplane—are reflected back to the radar transmitter location. By measuring the time it takes a pulse to travel out to the plane and back, one can determine the distance to the plane; the longer it takes the pulse to make the round-trip, the more distant the plane.

The Germans realized that if they transmitted false pulses, jamming the British radars, it would be difficult for the English to separate the real radar signals from the imposter signals. This would mean, of course, that it would become difficult to determine the distance, or even the presence, of German planes.

The British army hoped it could determine the source of the German jamming by setting up receiver stations specifically designed to intercept the jamming signals. In February 1942, one of the operators of this system noticed a peculiar thing. His receiver picked up a flood of radio noise that he could not account for. Puzzled by this observation, he was able to trace the strange noise to a solar eruption centered on a huge sunspot. The whole project, of course, was heavily classified; so nothing could be said about it at the time. But here was clear evidence that the sun, like the Milky Way, was broadcasting radio waves.

While the English were able to continue the development of radar and make related observations, the astronomers in the Netherlands, by now under German occupation, had to focus on theoretical work because they had no equipment at their disposal. One of the great puzzles produced by Jansky's and Reber's observations was the question: What generates the radio noise? Since it was known by then that there was a great deal of hydrogen in space, it seemed natural to try to determine how hydrogen might generate radio waves.

Just before the war ended in 1944, a young Dutch theorist predicted that hydrogen should generate radio noise at a frequency whose corresponding wavelength was twenty-one centimeters. He based his prediction on Bohr's model of the hydrogen atom. According to the Dutch theorist's prediction, however, a given atom would radiate at twenty-one centimeters only about once in every eleven million years. This is so because any particular atom can radiate only once as its electron jumps to a lower orbit. It cannot radiate again unless something happens—a collision with another hydrogen atom perhaps—to knock its electron into a higher orbit so that it can once again radiate at a later time. Space contains about one hydrogen atom per cubic centimeter—far less than the best vacuums ever produced on Earth. But in spite of this almost total vacuum in space, the universe is so enormous that the hydrogen radiation should be fairly easy to detect if the theory was correct.

After the war, the Dutch began to look for this radiation, using an antenna that belonged to the Post and Telegraph Service. Unfortunately, before they could make the crucial observation, their receiver caught fire; and before they got it repaired, the confirming observation was made in the United States by two Harvard scientists.

The discovery that Jupiter, like the sun and the Milky Way, emits radio waves is another example of an unexpected result from an experiment designed to study something else. In 1955, two scientists at the Carnegie Institution of Washington, Kenneth L. Franklin and Bernard Burke, were making plans to create a map of the radio sky at a frequency that was about one-third the frequency Reber had used in his first study. They used an antenna that detected radio waves from only a very small patch of the sky at a time. This meant that to complete their map, they had to make many observations over many days, pointing their antenna toward a new patch of sky with each observation so as to cover completely the part of the sky they were interested in.

An important part of any astronomical observation is what is called *calibration*. This means simply that the observer needs to have some way to make sure the equipment is not changing during the course of the experiment. For example, if you are measuring the brightness of a star over a period of many days, you want to make sure the lens on the telescope hasn't become smudged, thus leading you to believe that the star has become dimmer when in fact all that has happened is that the telescope lens has become dirty.

One way to calibrate a telescope is to look always at a star whose brightness you know. If the star is as bright as you know it should be, then you know the telescope is operating properly. If the star appears dimmer than it should be, then you know something is wrong with the telescope.

Franklin and Burke decided to calibrate their radio telescope by pointing it at the Crab Nebula, a known and reliable emitter of radio waves. The idea was to record the Crab Nebula sometime during each observation period to provide a calibration point. Beyond that, they didn't have much of an observation plan.

Franklin's recollection of the experiment appeared later in a book titled *Serendipitous Discoveries in Radio Astronomy,* and is worth quoting in part:

> . . . *Bernie said to me, "Ken, which way should it go?"*— *meaning the direction to point the antenna. Well, it is either north or south, you know; it's an arbitrary decision. And I said, "South." So we went south and continued to go south. . . . Once in a while we would get some interference. . . . I remember telling Bernie one day, "Hey, you know we have got to figure out what that thing is." He said, "I suppose so," and that was that.*
>
> *One Monday Bernie gathered up all the records with the interference on them. . . . "Ken, come in here," he said. "I*

want to show you something." He had taken all of these records and lined them up so that the Crab Nebula was in a nice straight line. And then we saw that the interference also roughly lined up. He said, "We've got something here!"

Howard Tatel (a friend) was in the laboratory. Howard Tatel was interested in all kinds of things. He was going over some seismic records because he was interested in the roots of mountains. He was also interested in the hydrogen distribution in the galaxy. I asked him one day, "Howard, how do you justify and bring all these things together?" "You're looking down and you're looking up," he said. "We live on a surface. I'm interested in anything that is off it!"

Then Howard said (about the interference we were looking at), "Maybe it's Jupiter." . . . So I went to the Almanac and looked at the position of Jupiter, and it was pretty close. I don't know how Howard came to that suggestion.*

A few weeks after Franklin and Burke had announced their discovery that Jupiter emitted radio waves, others confirmed their result. It was becoming evident that the visible universe was only the proverbial tip of the iceberg. There was a lot more to look at out there than would ever meet any eye.

The results of another "well-planned" experiment led to the discovery of pulsars by Jocelyn Bell, a young Irish astronomy student at Cambridge University in England. Bell had been assigned to a project directed toward studying the gas that streams continuously from the sun—the so-called *solar wind.* The idea was to point one of the Cambridge radio telescopes

---

*Kellerman, K., and B. Sheets, eds. *Serendipitous Discoveries in Radio Astronomy.* Green Bank, WV: National Radio Astronomy Observatory, 1983.

Jocelyn Bell
discovered pulsars.

toward a radio star, a star known to emit radio signals. As the solar wind streamed between the telescope on Earth and the radio star, it would cause the star to fluctuate in signal strength, in the same way that visible stars twinkle at night because of changes in Earth's atmosphere between Earth and the stars.

The fluctuations were recorded on a strip of paper three inches wide that unrolled at the rate of one hundred feet every day, seven days a week, for six months. It was Bell's job to examine the paper in minute detail for signs of radio star twinkling caused by the solar wind.

The radio telescope operated in such a way that it produced a rather peculiar pattern on the paper strip in the absence of solar-wind twinkling. "A small bump, a big bump, and a small bump, and that's it," as Bell described the pattern. The whole pattern taken together, as shown in Figure 1a, reminded Bell of a wartime cartoon character called Chad, who was usually seen peeping over a wall. In the United States, a similar character was named Kilroy, and was usually associated with the phrase, "Kilroy was here." During solar twinkling, Chad grew a mustache and eyebrows, so that he looked something like Figure 1b.

Recording a complete round of observations required about four hundred feet of paper, and then the process would start all over again. Bell noticed that there was, quite consistently, for every four hundred feet of paper, a small patch of radio noise about a quarter of an inch long, which she called scruff because it didn't look exactly like the solar twinkling. When she used a particular radio frequency to look at the scruff more carefully,

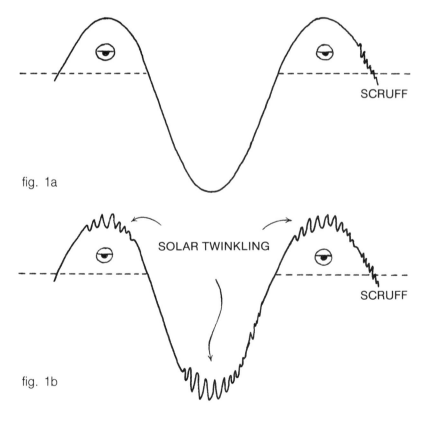

fig. 1a

SCRUFF

SOLAR TWINKLING

SCRUFF

fig. 1b

Bell discovered that it was in fact made up of a very regular pattern of pulses—one about every one-and-a-third seconds.

More investigation showed that the scruff always showed up in the same patch of sky during each round of observations. Bell pointed out the scruff to her thesis adviser, Tony Hewish, who later won a Nobel prize for his extensive observations and innovations in radio astronomy. "Yes, it's interesting," Hewish responded. "We must follow it up."

At first Hewish and Bell thought the scruff was man-made—caused perhaps by electrical interference from some nearby electric motor. But then they noticed that the scruff repeated itself at intervals of 23 hours and 56 minutes, not once every 24 hours, as one would expect if the noise was repeating itself on some man-made schedule.

The fact that the schedule was 4 minutes short of 24 hours was an important clue. A star is in the same position in the sky every night not every 24 hours, but every 23 hours and 56 minutes. The reason for this odd time interval is that as Earth spins on its axis once every 24 hours, it is also circling the sun once a year. The combination of these two motions produces the odd repetition pattern. It seemed clear, then, that the scruff was coming from outer space, because it moved in step with the stars. But no such regular radiation pattern had ever been seen before from a radio star. It had the look of a man-made transmission. "This is where this silly LGM notion came from," Bell explained. "If it's not Earth man made, maybe it's Little Green Men out there trying to signal us."

A few months later, Bell pointed her telescope, still tuned to the same radio frequency she'd used to study the scruff, toward another part of the sky. And here she discovered another bit of scruff with a series of pulses that repeated at intervals of 1.19

seconds. That discovery convinced her that LGMs were not responsible. "It was highly unlikely that two lots of Little Green Men on two different planets could choose the same radio frequency for their broadcast," she said, "and an unlikely technique to signal the same inconspicuous planet Earth!"

Later many more pulsating radio stars—*pulsars,* as they are called today—were discovered. As we shall see, pulsars are a natural part of the evolution that many stars go through in their transition from one stage to the next. But at the time they were discovered, no one had any good idea as to what these exotic stars might be.

For a time Bell was a celebrity. As she describes it: "I had my photograph taken standing on the bank [of a river], sitting on the bank, standing on the bank examining bogus records. One of them [reporters] even had me running down the bank waving my arms. 'Look happy, dear—you've just made a Discovery!' . . . They also asked me a number of relevant questions like: Was I taller than Princess Margaret, or not quite so tall? How many boyfriends did I have at once?"

As the radio astronomers made one exciting discovery after another, other scientists began to wonder about the possibility of looking at the universe through infrared and ultraviolet "colored glasses." We shall take up the infrared story next.

IRAS, Red Giants, and White Dwarfs

We have learned that radio, infrared, visible, ultraviolet, X-ray, and gamma-ray waves are all part of the electromagnetic spectrum. So we realize that Planck's radiation curve, which ranged from red on the low-frequency end to violet on the high-frequency end, is not the whole curve. And we now understand that the thermometers placed just below the red end of the spectrum were heated by electromagnetic waves in the infrared area; the silver salts placed just above the violet end of the spectrum were darkened by electromagnetic waves in the ultraviolet region. That is, infrared waves and ultraviolet waves are themselves part of the Planck radiation spectrum; so we should add them to the curve, as Figure 1 shows.

For similar reasons we have added, and placed in their proper positions along the Planck curve, the rest of the electromagnetic spectrum—the radio, X-ray, and gamma-ray parts. Now we see that any warm body emits the whole spectrum of radiation types, from radio waves on the low-frequency end to gamma rays on

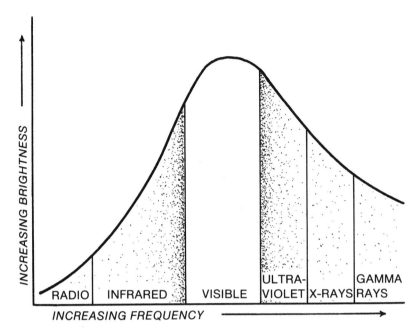

fig. 1

the high-frequency end. This means, of course, that if we examined the sun—or any star or other warm celestial body, for that matter—with the proper instruments, we would expect to find radiation at any frequency along the Planck curve.

But this expectation turns out not to be true; at least it is not true if we are observers on Earth's surface. We have already mentioned that harmful solar ultraviolet emissions are blocked by Earth's atmosphere. The same is also true of most infrared, X-ray, and gamma-ray waves. So if we wish to observe the universe at these frequencies, we need to get above part or most of Earth's atmosphere.

Before the first satellite was launched, some brief observations had been made from high-altitude balloons and rockets. And some useful observations were made and are still being made from the tops of mountains where a portion of Earth's atmosphere lies below the observers' feet. But the revolutionary results have been found, for the most part, by placing observing instruments in satellites and space probes well above Earth's atmosphere. These instruments are designed to collect gamma-ray, X-ray, radio-wave, and infrared radiations—in short, all of the kinds of radiation that reach Earth's surface only in very limited quantities if at all.

So, in a way, depending on the observation frequency, we can say that there are many different pictures of the universe—the gamma-ray picture, the X-ray picture, the radio picture, and so on. We can think of the universe as being many overlapping universes, and the one we see depends on our choice of observation frequency. Today's astronomers are often categorized by the region of the electromagnetic spectrum in which they make their observations. Thus we have radio astronomers, infrared astronomers, and so on. As we shall see in later chapters, the real nature of the universe begins to appear when we bring together the various pictures resulting from observations made at different frequencies.

Here we shall concentrate on the infrared picture. The American inventor and entrepreneur Thomas Alva Edison was the first of the infrared astronomers. In 1878, during an eclipse of the sun, Edison set up what we would today call an infrared detector, in a henhouse on a farm near Rawlins, Wyoming Territory. His observations clearly revealed that the sun emitted infrared radiation. Like Jansky's first observations of radio waves from the Milky Way, Edison's result received much attention in the press—partly because of Edison's superb ability to promote his own undertakings—which soon died away. It was only after the rapid succession of important results obtained by radio astronomers that scientists directed serious attention toward other seg-

Edison concocted this hornlike device as part of an instrument he called a Tasimeter. The horn focused infrared radiation on a sensitive instrument that measured temperature.

ments of the invisible part of the electromagnetic spectrum.

Although there have been many infrared observations with many different approaches in the last few decades, we shall discuss only the most singularly successful one of them all, the observations made with the Infrared Astronomical Satellite—the IRAS—launched early in 1983. The infrared instruments carried by the satellite operated successfully for about a year and revealed some 250,000 formerly unknown stars radiating strongly in the infrared part of the spectrum.

In our discussion of Planck's radiation curve we learned that the frequency at which the strongest radiation occurs depends on the temperature of the warm body. As temperature cools, the peak radiation shifts downward from the blue and green areas of the spectrum toward the color red. So we would expect relatively cool stars to have their strongest radiation in the red part

Technicians prepare IRAS for launch.

of the spectrum. And as we move to even cooler stars, the strongest radiation moves into the infrared—invisible—part of the spectrum. Thus the 250,000 stars detected by IRAS should represent a collection of largely cool stars. We say "should" because the correct interpretation is not always so simple.

As Figure 2 shows, the infrared part of the spectrum is not just one frequency, but rather a band of frequencies. It is customary to break the infrared part of the spectrum into three different sections. First we have the near infrared spectrum, which is the part nearest the red part of the visible spectrum. Then, as we move to lower frequencies, we have a section called middle infrared; and finally, the third section, called the far infrared. We can interpret the three parts in terms of temperature. Objects whose peak radiations are in the near infrared are hotter than objects whose peak radiations are in the middle infrared; and objects whose peak radiation are in the far infrared are the coolest of all.

As a rule of thumb, however, astronomers have been able to say more than this. Those objects that radiate strongly in the near infrared are usually stars. At a somewhat lower temperature, where radiation is strongest in the middle infrared, the emissions are generally due to a kind of hot dust. And finally, in the far infrared, at even cooler temperatures, the radiation is generally due to cold dust. So if we examined a particular object in all three sections of the infrared spectrum and discovered significant amounts of radiation in all three, we would suspect that we were looking at a star surrounded by both hot and cool dust. Let's see how we might apply this simple interpretation to the fifth brightest star in the nighttime sky, Vega.

Vega is in our own Milky Way galaxy, about twenty-six light-years away from the sun. That is, the light from Vega just now

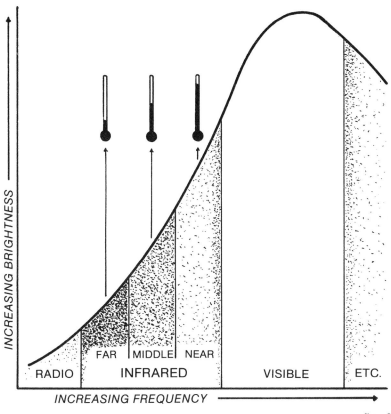

fig. 2

reaching our own solar system started its journey about twenty-six light-years ago. A light-year is about 5,865,696,000,000,000 miles. As stars go, Vega is pretty close. Some of the stars in our Milky Way galaxy are more than two hundred thousand light-years away, and other stars in more distant galaxies are millions and even billions of light-years away.

Since Vega is visible to the eye, we know that it emits its strongest radiation in the visible part of the Planck radiation curve, as Figure 3 shows. Observations in the near infrared also follow the Planck radiation curve, as the theory predicts. But as IRAS revealed, when observations are extended into the middle

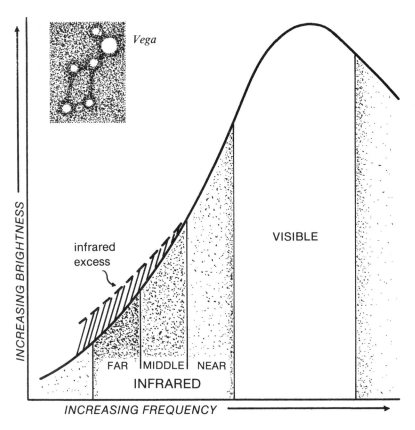

fig. 3

and far infrared part of the Planck curve, something peculiar happens. Instead of the curve dropping down, as it should according to Planck's theory, it flattens out, as the broken line indicates. There is an infrared excess.

What can we make of this situation? Well, as we said, strong infrared radiation in the middle and far infrared regions suggests some kind of dust. But what kind? Here the detective work starts.

Our first facts are that Vega is about two and a half times as massive as the sun and about fifty times as bright. It just looks dimmer because it is so far away. Let's see what this tells us about the size of the dust particles surrounding Vega. If the particles were the size of dust particles in our homes and smaller, they would have been blown away long ago by the radiation from Vega's hot surface. Because of a complex interaction involving Vega's gravitation and radiation fields, larger particles—up to about one millimeter in size—would have gone in the opposite direction; they would have spiraled into Vega's atmosphere and disappeared. So we can set a lower limit to the size of the dust particles at about one millimeter.

The fact that we get a significant amount of radiation in the near and far infrared means that there are not just a few big particles—or in the extreme case, a single planet—revolving around Vega. A few big particles would not have enough surface area to generate the observed infrared radiation. So we are left with a large number of pea-sized grains to explain the observed radiation.

These infrared observations are the very first compelling evidence, ever, that another star besides our sun is surrounded by solid matter. Vega is a much younger star than the sun, so it may be that the grains surrounding Vega will in time condense under their mutual gravitational attraction into a system of planets. But we need to understand much more than we do now about planetary formation to make such a prediction with certainty.

Since the discovery of the grains around Vega, about fifty other stars with similar infrared excess have been detected. The findings suggest that these too may be stars in an early stage of planetary development.

If infrared observations have perhaps revealed the early stages of the birth of planetary systems, we can say with more certainty that such observations have allowed us a glimpse of both the birth and death of stars. Here and there throughout the universe we find relatively dense regions of cold dust and gas—for the most part hydrogen and helium. Some of these regions are denser than others, and in some cases the density is enough so that the region, because of the mutual gravitational attraction between the gas and dust particles, begins to collapse into a ball—the initial stage of a star. As the ball collapses, the mutual self-gravitation grows even stronger, and the star begins to heat up.

At this stage the star is still surrounded by a cloud of gas, so we cannot see it directly. But what we can see is the infrared radiation from the gas surrounding the star. The gas radiates because it is being heated by the star hidden inside the gas shroud. The photo on page 65, released in June of 1989, shows a star-forming cloud observed by an infrared telescope located on Kitt Peak, near Tucson, Arizona. The star, 2,400 light-years from Earth in the constellation Cepheus, is well within our Milky Way galaxy. In this image we cannot see the star itself. What we do see are infrared emissions from hydrogen molecules in the cloud heated to a temperature near 2,000 degrees by a high-speed stellar wind emanating from a newly emerging star buried deeply in the shroud.

Given enough time, the star may move out of the cloud and the gas shroud may condense into the pea-sized grains of the kind surrounding Vega. If this happens, the star finally reveals itself.

This process takes thousands and millions of years, of course; so no one during a single lifetime would ever see a star form from a condensing cloud of gas and dust and then finally appear. What we can see, however, by looking at many different places in the sky, are stars in various stages of development. The

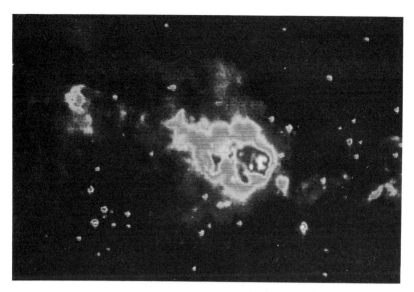

This infrared photograph of a star-forming cloud in Cepheus was taken by Adair P. Lane and John Bally.

situation is somewhat like walking through a redwood forest to understand the life cycle of redwood trees. Redwood trees live many hundreds of years, so no one individual could ever follow the life of a single tree from birth to death. But we can study many redwood trees in various stages of development, from seedling to young tree to mature tree, and so on. In this way we can piece together the life history of a redwood tree.

As a young star continues to collapse, its pressure and the temperature in its center finally reach the point where nuclear reactions start. First the hydrogen, the lightest of all the elements, in the star "burns," producing helium, the second lightest element; then the helium burns, producing carbon and oxygen. Then the carbon and oxygen burn, producing heavier elements, and so on, until the burning reaches some final stage. So it is in the interior of stars that many of the heavier elements are forged from the elemental hydrogen and helium created during the Big Bang. The Big Bang is the generally accepted theory that the universe began with a violent eruption from an initial, very compact state of enormous density. All matter, space, and time presumably evolved and expanded from this initial explosion.

Just what the final burning stage of a star is depends almost exclusively on its initial mass. The most massive stars end their nuclear burning stage with iron. But for a star like our sun, a rather ordinary star in the scheme of things, the burning stops just before it reaches the carbon-oxygen burning stage. As the burning approaches this limit, the star balloons into a huge, relatively cool red ball of gas with a diameter that would engulf the most distant planets in our solar system. In this ballooned stage, the star is called a *red giant*; the red glow in its outer shroud of gas is produced by the heat generated in the inner core of the star. As we might expect, measurements in the infrared region are ideal for studying the relatively cool gas surrounding the stellar core. The gas is cool because of its great distance from the hot core.

For stars like our own sun, the red-giant stage is the next to the last stage in their evolution. In the final stage, when all the nuclear fuel in the star's core has been exhausted, the star collapses on itself and forms what is called a *white dwarf*. At this stage the star is so dense that a teaspoonful of it would weigh as much as a bus. From this point on, the white dwarf gradually cools, becoming, finally, a cinder in space. This is the fate of our sun. See Figure 4.

It is appropriate here to say a bit about the nature of scientific explanation and reasoning. Some scientific results are little more than a statement of a direct observation: Earth has one moon, and the planet Saturn is surrounded by rings. These are results

fig. 4

we can observe directly or determine with even the most modest telescope.

Other results spring from a mixture of observation and theory. The notion that pea-sized grains surround Vega is a good example. We observe the infrared excess directly, with sophisticated instruments; but then we infer indirectly that the excess is produced by grains surrounding the star. This inference, we recall, depended on our knowledge of the mass and brightness of Vega. With this basic information, in conjunction with our understanding of gravity and the interaction of Vega's radiation with particles of various sizes, we could then conclude that the particles had some lower size limit. On the other hand, we used our knowledge of the radiation and reflection properties of particles versus their size to conclude that the particles must have some upper size limit. The true particle size, then, must lie between these allowed upper and lower limits.

As we continue our investigation of the universe we shall find that, more and more, we move away from the results observed by direct observation and toward a combination of observation and theory. Next we shall look at the layer of our universe revealed by observation in the ultraviolet and higher regions of the electromagnetic spectrum.

7

Explosions, Ice Balls, and Black Holes

Throughout history, poets and scholars have expressed mankind's concept of the universe in such phrases as "harmony of the heavens," "music of the spheres," and "celestial clockwork." To the unaided eye, and even with the sophisticated telescopes of the twentieth century, the universe presents a stability observed nowhere else in nature. The unchanging constellations parading across the sky each night and the precise predictability of eclipses of the sun and moon suggest a universe more like the vault of a vast, immutable, celestial cathedral than a stage for the most unimaginably violent processes in nature.

Only occasionally is the stability of the visible nighttime sky disrupted by a faint meteor trail or the infrequent appearance of a comet. And only on the rarest of the most rare occasions does the sky present a truly unexpected event—a *supernova*—an exploding star bright enough for the naked eye to see.

The most famous supernova in history occurred in the ninth century and was described in 1054 in a Chinese document, the

"Chinese Annals." At its brightest, the supernova was as clearly visible as Venus in the nighttime sky. Today all that is left to the naked eye is a faintly glowing star.

Much to the delight of astronomers and to the wonder of the general public, a spectacular supernova has occurred in our own time. In February 1987, headlines around the world proclaimed that astronomers in the Southern Hemisphere had observed an "exploding star" in a small galaxy of stars, the Large Magellanic Cloud, near our own Milky Way galaxy. This is perhaps the most studied event in the history of astronomy, and because of its significance we shall devote the entire chapter following this one to it alone.

But supernovas are not the only strange or violent events in the universe. Novas, or exploding stars that can be seen with powerful telescopes, are fairly common. They are smaller than supernovas and are too far away to be studied in detail. But there are other exhibits in our vast celestial museum whose stellar wonders are as bizarre and strange as any ever seen, or perhaps ever imagined, on Earth. Let's examine some of these.

We know by now that a blackbody radiates in accord with the Planck radiation curve; as we move to warmer and warmer bodies, the maximum, or peak, radiation occurs at higher and higher frequencies. We also know that temperature is one measure of the energy associated with a body. We need to say a little more about the energy-temperature connection here.

If we looked at a warm substance—say hydrogen gas enclosed inside a glass container—with a sufficiently powerful microscope—which doesn't exist, of course—we would see that the atoms of hydrogen making up the gas were moving around in a random way, occasionally colliding with one another. If we heated the gas, we would see that the average speed of the hydrogen atoms increased as long as we continued to apply heat, and that the rate at which the atoms collided with each other also increased, as Figure 1 shows. So we can think of the temperature of a gas as telling us something about the average speed of atoms in the gas: the higher the temperature, the greater the average speed of the atoms.

We also know that energy and speed are related. A car traveling at one hundred miles an hour has more energy of motion— *kinetic energy*, as it is called—than does a car moving at two miles an hour. In a similar way, the kinetic energy of the hydrogen atoms in our glass container increases as the average speed of the atoms increases. Since temperature is a measure of the average speed of the atoms, we see that temperature is also a measure of the kinetic energy of the gas. If we put all of this together, we realize that as we look at hotter and hotter stars, we are also looking at more and more energetic stars.

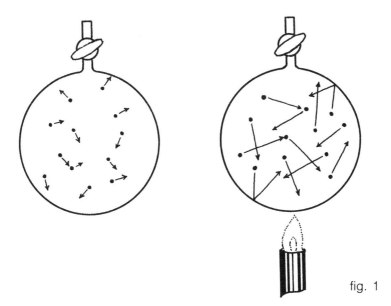

fig. 1

We can interpret this connection in terms of the Planck radiation curve. As we move to increasingly more energetic stars, the peak of the Planck radiation curve for these stars moves to increasingly higher frequencies. So a star whose peak radiation frequency is in the ultraviolet part of the spectrum is a hotter, more energetic star than is one whose peak frequency is in the visible spectrum.

Quite often we can extend this observation to say that the more energetic the process, the higher the frequency of the strongest radiation associated with that process. So if we are observing almost any process in the universe that generates radiation—not just blackbody radiation from a star described by the Planck curve—we can generally say that the frequency of the predominant radiation is a good clue to the energy—or violence—of the process.

This is another example of seeing different parts and processes in the universe depending on the radiation frequency at which we are making our observations. For instance—although we are getting ahead of our story a bit—strong infrared radiation suggests a star that is peacefully approaching the last stages of its evolutionary path, whereas strong X rays coming from some direction in the sky suggest a violent process—perhaps two stars sideswiping each other.

So let's focus now on what ultraviolet, X-ray, and gamma-ray waves have revealed to us about the universe. Since these waves are at the high-frequency end of the electromagnetic spectrum, we would expect to be exploring the most energetic, and as it turns out, sometimes the most violent processes in nature.

As we have mentioned, Earth's atmosphere shields its surface from ultraviolet, X-ray, and gamma-ray radiation. And so, as with infrared radiation, the best observations in the high-frequency end of the electromagnetic spectrum have been made with satellites and space probes well above Earth's atmosphere. Many such observations have been made in the last few decades. Scientists have used everything from rockets that arched above Earth's atmosphere for only a few moments to observations from manned platforms circling Earth. We shall touch on only a few observations that exemplify the results from the many different projects.

On June 26, 1978, the Inter Ultraviolet Explorer satellite (the IUE) was launched from the Kennedy Space Center. This satellite was first conceived by a British astronomer in the late 1960s and was finally launched under the auspices of the United States National Aeronautics and Space Administration (NASA), the European Space Agency, and the British Science and Engineering Research Council. This was an example of how the scientific community often undertakes a complicated scientific mission in a spirit of cooperation and mutual interest that seems difficult to achieve in the political world.

The IUE has been, by most counts, the most successful astronomical satellite ever launched. Designed to work for three years, it still continues to operate more than ten years later. Furthermore, the important and wide-ranging results obtained from the IUE cover a who's who of the celestial family. We can give here only a taste of what the observations have achieved. We'll consider first those occasional visitors to our neighborhood, the comets.

Astronomers often refer to comets as "dirty snowballs." Early theories proposed that comets were made up mostly of frozen water and dust. And IUE and other related observations have largely confirmed that this description is fairly accurate. Information about the amount of water escaping from a comet as it approaches and is heated by the sun can be gleaned from certain ultraviolet radiations emitted by the water in the head of the

comet. By measuring the strength of these radiations, astronomers have been able to study how the composition of a comet changes in its journey through the solar system.

Just recently, in the spring of 1987, studies made in Europe and Canada have added support to an interesting but controversial theory that the water that fills Earth's oceans comes from "blackened snowballs that fall from space by the millions." University of Iowa physicist Louis A. Frank first proposed the theory. While examining ultraviolet images collected by the *Dynamics Explorer I* satellite to study air glow around Earth from 1981 to 1986, Frank found unexpected holes punched through Earth's atmosphere. After considering various explanations, he concluded that the holes could be made only by "space snowballs"—one-hundred-ton comets made of ice coated with black hydrocarbons—which are falling into Earth's atmosphere at a rate of ten million a year.

The ice balls, according to the theory, disintegrate and become vapor in Earth's atmosphere. The vapor falls as rain and becomes part of Earth's water cycle. Frank calculated that the ice balls, measuring about thirty feet in diameter, would contribute about one inch of water all over Earth's surface every ten thousand years. If this has been going on during the 4.5 billion years since Earth's formation, the process would have provided enough water to fill all of our oceans and form the polar ice packs.

To return to the IUE observations of comets, the dust in a comet reflects the ultraviolet light from the sun; so by studying this radiation, astronomers have been able to learn more about the properties of the dust in comets' heads. Perhaps the most

An artist's concept of the IUE transmitting information to science laboratories in Greenbelt, Maryland, and Madrid, Spain.

important finding of their observations of this dust is that comets seem to be made of the stuff that surrounded the sun during the early days of planetary formation. So by studying comets we are learning about the composition of our solar system at its very beginning.

Since the sun is our nearest star, we know a good deal more about it than we know about any of the other stars. In our discussion of the discovery of pulsars, we pointed out that the discovery was the result of a fortuitous accident; the primary goal of the experiment was to study the stream of gas and particles that blows continuously away from the sun—the solar wind. An interesting question is, Do other stars also have similar winds?

Hot stars radiate most strongly in ultraviolet frequencies, whereas our sun radiates most strongly in the visible part of the spectrum. Since IUE measurements are confined to the ultraviolet part of the spectrum, we would expect this satellite to give us the most information about the hot stars—stars at least twice as hot as our sun.

The data from IUE show that almost all hot stars do have stellar winds. These winds have much greater density and move at much higher speeds than the winds from the sun—not too surprising, perhaps. The surprise is that the temperatures of the hot-star winds are cooler than the temperature of the solar wind from our sun. Why this is true is not known.

Solar and stellar winds are created by the pressure of the radiation from the star's hot surface. The intense radiation from this surface drives away the gases lying above it. Although the rate at which a star loses material via the stellar wind is slight— typically a few millionths of the star's total mass each year—the cumulative effect of the loss should have, over many millions of years, a significant impact on the star's evolution. Because stellar winds are such a new discovery, however, little is known about just what this impact might be.

IUE has also revealed important information about our own sun. An outstanding problem for solar astronomers has to do with the temperature of the atmosphere surrounding the sun. The sun's atmosphere consists of two parts: an inner atmosphere called the *chromosphere,* and an outer atmosphere called the corona. The peculiar thing is that the chromosphere is several times hotter than the sun's surface, and the corona is even hotter; it is more than ten times hotter than the sun's surface. It is as though, when we ascend into our own atmosphere, we find that the temperature gets hotter as we go up, instead of cooler. See Figure 2.

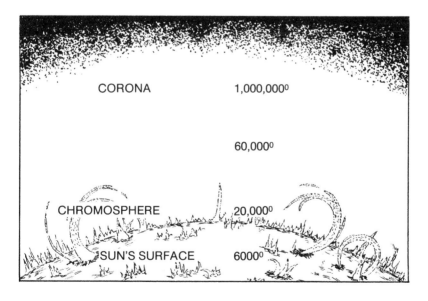

fig. 2

We can be a little more specific about this problem. We know that the heat energy generated by the sun comes from an intensely hot region in its center created by continual hydrogen-bomblike nuclear explosions. The heat flows away from the very hot center toward the cooler surface. This is what we expect; heat flows from warmer bodies to cooler bodies. (If this were not true, it would do no good to build a fire in a fireplace.)

But then the heat energy flowing from the sun's center reaches the lower part of the chromosphere, the sun's inner atmosphere, where it encounters a temperature increase. We know that the energy from the sun's center has to escape eventually from the sun; otherwise, the sun would heat up indefinitely and finally explode. How, then, does this energy flow through the ever increasing rise in temperature that it encounters as it passes first through the chromosphere and then through the even hotter corona?

One suggestion was that the energy was carried through the sun's inner and outer atmospheres by stupendous sound waves. But these predictions have not been born out by IUE observations. The IUE is helpful in these observations because the chromosphere and corona, being much hotter than the sun, are strong emitters in the ultraviolet region—just the region the IUE was designed to study.

If solar sound waves are not the answer, then what other answer might there be? It seems likely that the sun's magnetic field plays an important role. The suggestion is that there is something like a colossal electric power generating plant that transports the necessary energy through the sun's atmosphere in spite of the progressively hotter temperature of the chromosphere and corona. The magnetic field needed to generate the electric power is created by the rotation of the sun.

This explanation suggests that stars rotating faster than our sun should have stronger ultraviolet emissions from their atmosphere than does the sun. And this is exactly what IUE has revealed. And thus, by studying other stars, we have been able to learn more about our own sun.

The idea of studying other stars to learn more about the sun brings up an interesting, somewhat philosophical issue regarding the status of astronomy as a science in the normal sense of the word. In most scientific endeavors, an experiment is proposed to test some theory. The experiment can be repeated over and over under many different, well-defined conditions. If the experiment bears out the predictions of the theory, then we feel justified in using the theory. Furthermore, by carrying out the experiment in a wide variety of controlled conditions, we gain some information about the general validity of the theory.

But there is only one universe. We cannot try out theories in a variety of universes to test their range of validity. Furthermore, we can't very well do experiments on the one universe we have. We can't create a star in the laboratory to see what happens, as we can a new chemical compound.

It appeared, until recently, that the best we could do was to study, as well as we could, the bewildering array of phenomena provided by the universe in the hope that we might discover some common theme or themes wrapping the universe into a unified whole. But as we shall see in the Epilogue to this book, there may be more to the story.

Now let's move up in frequency to the X-ray rung of the electromagnetic ladder. This frequency range provides us with a window into the universe at its most violent.

The first X-ray pictures of the universe were obtained in 1948 from relatively crude instruments sent up in captured V-2 German rockets. They did little more than reveal the existence of X rays in space. Somewhat later, again with rockets, scientists discovered the source of X rays to be the sun. As we might suspect from our earlier discussion of ultraviolet emissions, the X rays were coming from the hottest part of the sun's atmosphere, the corona.

The next big discovery in X-ray astronomy occurred, as so often happens, while the experimenters were looking for something else. Some scientists believed that the moon should be a source of weak X rays, even though the moon itself is relatively cool. The theory was that energetic particles from the sun would bounce off the moon, producing X rays in the process.

An X-ray detector launched to look for these moon-born X rays discovered, instead, X rays coming from a direction almost opposite to that of the moon. Further investigation showed that the X rays were coming from a source lying in the constellation Scorpius. More observations disclosed even more X-ray sources. It was hard to imagine how even the hottest of stars could emit such strong X-ray radiation. The results called for some radical, new kind of radiation mechanism.

In order to study these strange X-ray-emitting objects for hours and days at a time, scientists placed instruments aboard satellites. The first of these satellites discovered several hundred X-ray sources, the strongest of which were often double stars—that is, a system of two stars rotating around each other. Such stars, called *binary stars,* are common in the visible universe, but what was unusual about the X-ray-emitting binaries was that one of the two stars was always exceedingly small and dense.

Here was, in fact, the clue to unraveling the mystery of the X-ray emitters. The small star was so dense that its gravity was dragging material from the larger star onto itself. This process is so violent that the material streaming toward the small star becomes compressed and heats up to millions of degrees—more than hot enough to emit strong X rays, as Figure 3 shows.

It was clear by now that not only are stars sometimes violent by themselves—a nova, for example—but they can have violent interactions with each other and produce X rays in the process, one of the most lethal radiations known to man.

Most of the dense stars in these X-ray-producing binaries are what are called *neutron* stars. They are closely related to the white dwarf stars we discussed earlier. We learned that white dwarfs are the last stage in the evolution of some stars that first balloon into red giants and then collapse into white dwarfs when all their nuclear fuel is exhausted. Neutron stars are simply stars that are initially more massive than those that evolve into white

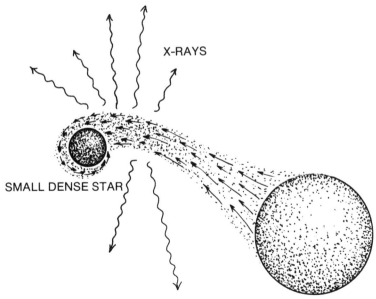

fig. 3

dwarfs. Instead, because of their extra mass, they collapse under their own gravity into stars even more dense than white dwarfs.

At this extreme density, the electrons circling the nuclei of the atoms that make up the stellar mass are pushed into the very core of the atom. When this happens, the positive core is neutralized by the crushed-in negative electrons. Now we have particles called *neutrons*—*neu* because they are electrically neutral—making up the material of the star; thus the name neutron star.

Some X-ray binaries, however, contain stars even more massive than neutron stars. Scientists established this fact from the rate at which the large star in the binary system circled its dense partner. The peculiar thing was that the dense partner was invisible. Here at last might be what scientists had predicted and called a *black hole.*

Black holes are the final evolutionary stage of stars that start out with even greater mass than the ones that turn into neutron stars. The electrons in neutron stars are crushed into the core of the atom under the tremendous self-gravity of the star; even more massive stars with their even greater self-gravity collapse into a kind of knot in space and time from which even light cannot escape. Furthermore, any object or material that comes near a black hole will be sucked into it and will disappear from view forever. See Figure 4. It is this material from the companion star streaming into a black hole that produces the strong X-ray emission.

Before concluding our discussion of high-frequency emissions, we must say something about the waves at the highest frequency, and therefore the most energetic end, of the electromagnetic spectrum—gamma rays. Strong bursts of gamma rays in outer space have been observed since 1973, but for all practi-

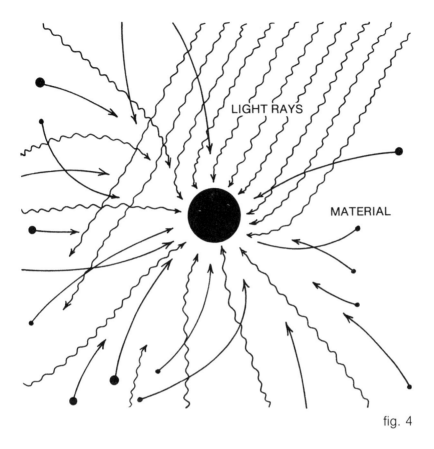

LIGHT RAYS

MATERIAL

fig. 4

cal purposes the origin of these bursts is not known. As of 1987, about twenty-five sources of gamma rays had been located, but only four of these had been identified with sources located by other means, such as through radio and X-ray observations. Many theories abound, often identifying gamma-ray sources with pulsars and black holes. But at the present time, all suggestions are little more than speculation.

Now we shall see how all the techniques of modern astronomy, from radio to X-ray observations, have been brought to bear on the most spectacular astronomical event in our time, the star that exploded in the Large Magellanic Cloud in 1987.

Once upon a Time, 170,000 Years Ago . . .

In 1520 Ferdinand Magellan cruised peacefully in the southern Pacific. It was his historic first voyage around the world. One of the crew scanning the nighttime sky later described what he saw: "Many small stars congregated . . . like two clouds." Today we call these clouds the Small Magellanic Cloud and the Large Magellanic Cloud in honor of the circumstances of their discovery by the Western world.

One hundred seventy thousand years ago, during the Old Stone Age on Earth, a dramatic event took place in the Large Magellanic Cloud. The explosion of a star twenty times more massive than our sun released enough energy to power every one of the one hundred billion stars in our Milky Way for several years. But no one knew about this explosion until February 23, 1987.

The Large Magellanic Cloud is a group of stars somewhat like our Milky Way galaxy but containing fewer stars. It's not large enough to be a galaxy and lacks the correct structure. It is some

The Large Magellanic Cloud, in which Sanduleak exploded 170,000 years ago, is visible only from the Southern Hemisphere.

170,000 light-years away, and that is why no one knew of the star's explosion until 170,000 years after it happened.

Nothing makes a scientific theory more believable than for it to predict something never seen before, and then for that prediction to come true. Einstein's general theory of relativity, which predicted, among other things, that starlight would be bent by a certain amount as it passed near the sun, is a spectacular example. Exactly what Einstein predicted was later found to be true, and Einstein and his general theory of relativity became famous.

Somewhat the same thing may be said for theories about the explosions of stars—the novas and supernovas. A considerable body of theory was and is available—the contributions of many scientists welded into a fairly coherent whole. But there have been very few observations to check against the detailed predictions of the body of theory. It is true that astronomers detect about one exploding star every two months, but the stars are at distances so great that it is impossible to see in detail what has happened. The thing that set the supernova in the Large Magellanic Cloud apart from others was that it happened, relatively speaking, in our own backyard.

Most supernovas that we detect are in galaxies millions and billions of light-years away. The Large Magellanic Cloud is the large group of stars nearest our Milky Way galaxy. So here at last was an unparalleled opportunity to check theory against observation.

As we know from our discussion of the Bohr model of the atom, a single hydrogen atom consists of a dense central core, the nucleus, with positive electrical charge, circled by a single electron whose negative electrical charge is equal and opposite to the charge on the nucleus. If we remove the electron from the hydrogen atom, the positive nucleus that is left is called a *proton.*

One of the theories of modern physics that attempts to bring together all of the forces in nature under one umbrella predicts that protons, given enough time, spontaneously decay into other subatomic particles, including one called a *neutrino.* Neutrinos pass unnoticed, by the millions, through our bodies every second. So it is not impossible to catch one, but neither is it easy.

Because the theory predicting that decaying protons produce neutrinos seems so compelling, considerable work has gone into building devices over the past few years to detect neutrinos. These devices are surprisingly simple. They consist of gigantic tubs of many thousands of tons of water—big enough for scuba divers to swim in—located deep underground. They are put underground so that they cannot be triggered by spurious events like cosmic rays. The idea is that occasionally a proton will spontaneously decay, producing a neutrino that will interact with the water to produce a small flash of light. The tub is surrounded by an array of cameralike devices ever ready to detect a flash of light.

To date no flash of light *from a decaying proton* had ever been detected. But on February 23, 1987, at 2 hours, 35 minutes, and 41 seconds, as scientist keep universal time, a total of nineteen flashes of light were detected in two different tubs of water—one located in Ohio and the other in Japan. As one astronomer said later, "These observations, without doubt, were made with the strangest telescope of all time." The neutrinos were detected some three hours before the supernova in the Large Magellanic Cloud was first detected visibly.

The general outline of a theory to explain supernovas first appeared in the 1930s. The suggestion was that a heavy star, ten or more times heavier than the sun, becomes unstable as it nears the end of its life. Several things happen during this unstable period. The core of the star collapses and packs the atoms so closely together that a neutron star forms. This much we have already discussed.

The neutron star is so dense that it may be only twelve miles in diameter—shrinking from an initial diameter fifty or more times that of the sun. As the core of the star collapses, the temperature and pressure inside rise dramatically. This causes the particles inside the core to crash into each other at tremendous speeds.

The crashing produces many other particles—most of them trapped by surrounding gases. But the neutrinos, which interact very little with matter, escape during the earliest moments of the stellar explosion. See Figure 1. They carry away more than 99.99 percent of the energy of the exploding star, and it is the relatively small amount of remaining energy that accounts for the appearance of the star in the visible and other parts of the electromagnetic spectrum.

Thus, according to theory, a supernova should first announce its presence by the escaping neutrinos. And as we have just said, neutrinos were detected some three hours before the visual appearance of the supernova in the Large Magellanic Cloud; the

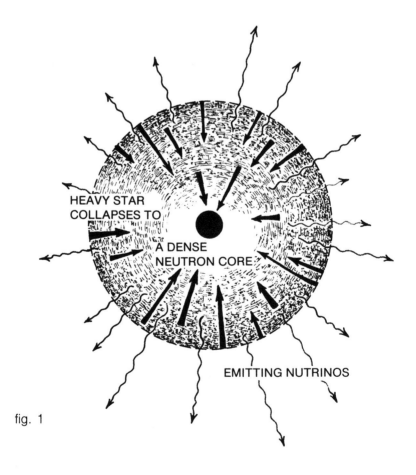

HEAVY STAR
COLLAPSES TO

A DENSE
NEUTRON CORE

EMITTING NUTRINOS

fig. 1

theory was further supported by the fact that the smidgen of neutrinos that were snagged was about what the theory had predicted.

The theorists are divided on what produces the expanding fireball that was first seen some three hours after the neutrinos arrived on Earth. As the star collapses, why doesn't it collapse totally, into a neutron star, instead of blasting off its outer layers and producing a brilliant light millions of times brighter than the sun?

One theory is that an outer layer of gas is blasted away from the star by the vast swarm of neutrinos escaping from the star's collapsing core. Another theory proposes that the core does not collapse uniformly; the interior of the core rapidly becomes a neutron star, and the outer layers of the core smash into it. This creates a bouncing action, forming a shock wave that drives outward and rips away the outer layers of the star in the process.

Whatever the explanation is, the collapsing star sends a blast of energy through the star's surface, heating the surrounding gases to a temperature of 100,000 degrees or more. At this temperature we would expect a gigantic flash of ultraviolet and X-ray radiation. Unfortunately, the satellites that might have detected this flash were not pointed in the right direction at the time of the supernova. But within a day the satellites had been redirected, and they easily detected ultraviolet and X-ray emissions from the dying fireball.

Photographs taken of the Large Magellanic Cloud before the supernova indicated that a star named Sanduleak-69 202 was the star that exploded. These earlier observations showed that Sanduleak was a hot star with a surface temperature of about 20,000 degrees, and a mass, as we said earlier, about twenty times that of the sun.

Sanduleak was a relatively young star when it exploded, about 20 million years old, compared to the sun's 5,000 million years. For about 95 percent of its life, the star burned hydrogen in its core, producing helium. Large stars like Sanduleak don't last as long as smaller stars like the sun. This is because the rate at which nuclear reactions take place in a star's interior increases with the mass of the star. So the bigger the star, the shorter its life.

About one million years ago, Sanduleak used up all of its hydrogen, and, following the sequence we discussed in Chapter 6, its resulting helium core began to shrink as the hydrogen furnace went cold. But as the star collapsed under its enormous weight, pressure began to heat the helium. Finally it reached a temperature where it could start to burn, turning the helium into carbon.

The temperature of the core was about 50 million degrees, and at this temperature the outer layers began to swell, producing a super red giant star hundreds of times larger than the sun. Some of the gas in the swollen layer was so distant from the star's center that gravity could not hold it, and so it was swept out into space by the stellar wind.

Apparently enough of the gas was lost in this manner so that the star shrank back to a giant blue-hot star some fifty times the diameter of the sun. For a while the fact that Sanduleak was a blue giant just before it exploded caused some concern among astronomers. Most stars are red giants, not blue-hot stars, just before they explode. But the stellar wind explanation, coupled with the fact that Sanduleak was somewhat smaller than most stars that become supernovas, seems to have convinced most astronomers that there are no real problems with the theory.

In any case, the star continued to burn helium in its core until the core turned to carbon. Again as the helium furnace went out, the star began to collapse until its core reheated to the point where carbon began to burn into neon. The carbon-burning phase lasted only about a thousand years. Then the center began to shrink and heat again until the carbon began to turn to silicon—a phase that lasted only about a year.

The star then started its last available stage—burning silicon into iron. Beyond iron no burning is possible. In fact, to create elements heavier than iron requires energy from an external source, whereas the fusion of elements lighter than iron produces energy.

The silicon-burning stage lasted only a few days. The star was now in a desperate situation. There was no inner energy source to keep it from collapsing under its own weight. If we could have sliced through the star at this point, a cross section would have looked like so many layers of an onion. At the center would be the star's iron core, surrounded in succession by shells of silicon, neon, carbon, and helium. The total mass amounted to about six suns. The outermost layer was a shell consisting mainly of hydrogen—hydrogen still unchanged from the time when the star was born.

The rest we have already described. Once the last nuclear furnace had gone out, the star collapsed catastrophically, creating a flood of neutrinos, followed by a flash of light that began to fade rapidly within a day or two.

How do we know what happened after the spectacular explosion? For an answer let's look at what happened here on Earth in the months after Sanduleak's collapse. Here we shall see how observations across the electromagnetic spectrum have helped us follow Sanduleak's postcollapse career.

We should expect that Sanduleak, like most stars, had a

stellar wind—even just before its collapse. The fireball blast wave quickly passed through the particles of gas in this stellar wind, producing weak radio signals that were detected on Earth in the first few days after the blast. Later on, this blast wave should catch up with the fossil debris left over from the red-giant stage in the star's life. This might happen any time soon, or it might happen years from now, with possibly dramatic results, such as strong radio emissions.

In May following the explosion, scientists found emission lines from nitrogen gas. These lines are more evidence that material from the red-giant stage is still in Sanduleak's vicinity. We would expect the gas from the red-giant stage to be rich in nitrogen, and the appearance of the nitrogen lines probably is due to the ultraviolet radiation portion of the fireball interacting with the nitrogen gas.

One of the interesting things about Sanduleak is the way its brightness in the visible spectrum has evolved since the fireball stage. In some ways it has not followed what is normally expected when a giant hot star explodes. First its brightness increased and decreased more rapidly than was expected. To some extent, this is probably due to the fact that Sanduleak originally was somewhat smaller than most supernovas.

Then after the supernova's initial flash of light, it began to increase again in brightness. The first few weeks of this strengthening glow can be explained by the energy released to the star's outer layers as the blast wave expanded outward. But after the blast wave had passed, the glow should have died down again. It didn't. It continued to grow, finally reaching its maximum in May and June of 1987 and slowly tapering off after that, as Figure 2 shows.

Surprisingly enough, what had happened is already pretty well understood. As the core collapsed, nuclear reactions pro-

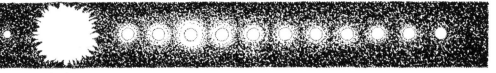

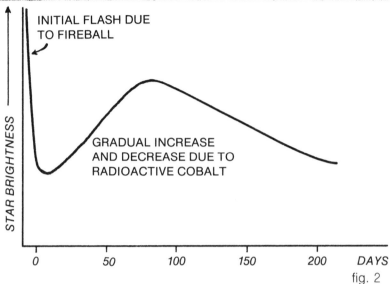

INITIAL FLASH DUE
TO FIREBALL

GRADUAL INCREASE
AND DECREASE DUE TO
RADIOACTIVE COBALT

STAR BRIGHTNESS

0   50   100   150   200   DAYS

fig. 2

duced a large amount of a radioactive form of nickel. This particular form of nickel has a half-life of about six days. That is, it takes about six days for half the original amount of nickel to decay radioactively into a radioactive form of cobalt. The cobalt, with a half-life of about eighty days, changes in turn to a stable form of iron.

As the cobalt decays into iron, it emits gamma rays, the rays at the high-frequency, most energetic end of the electromagnetic spectrum. It is these gamma rays that power the star after the shock wave has passed beyond the star's outer atmosphere. As Figure 2 shows, the width of the broad peak in the brightness-versus-time curve of the star, following the initial flash, is roughly equal to the half-life of cobalt. That is, after eighty days or so, enough of the cobalt had turned to iron so that the star began to dim again.

We might expect to see strong gamma rays during this period, but in fact we do not. The reason is that the gamma rays interact strongly with the material surrounding the center of the star and so cannot make their way directly to Earth. What happens instead is that the gamma rays gradually weaken, becoming the visible light whose variation we see in Figure 2, as well as weak X rays. These X rays were in fact detected by a Japanese satellite equipped with X-ray detectors and also by Soviet scientists aboard the Soviet Mir space station.

Figure 2 also shows us something else interesting: Scientists have been able to calculate, from the rate the curve has fallen off since its maximum, just how much radioactive nickel was produced during the explosion. The amount turns out to be equivalent to about 0.07 percent of the total mass of the sun. Here again is an example of how we can infer some result by using a combination of theory and observation—as we inferred that pea-sized particles surround Vega.

In February of 1989, Sanduleak presented a new face—one not altogether unexpected. In addition to the fading light we have just described, astronomers detected regular flashes of light—the signature of a pulsar. Pulsars, we recall, are the pulsating stars accidentally discovered by Jocelyn Bell in her search for solar wind.

According to theory, pulsars are the end result of the collapse of giant stars like Sanduleak. When such stars collapse into neutron stars, they decrease in size, as we have already said, to just a few tens of miles. Like the skater who pulls in her arms to increase the speed of her spin, a spinning star also speeds up dramatically as it shrinks in size. A typical neutron star might spin about its axis at the rate of many revolutions per second. But where do the pulses that Bell discovered come from?

Most stars, like Earth, have a magnetic field. In neutron stars this magnetic field rotates with the star. Electrically charged particles are swept along by the magnetic field. At great distances from the star, the electrons are moving along at enormous speeds, close to the speed of light, like the ice skater on the end of a crack-the-whip chain. At these speeds, electrons radiate enormous amounts of energy. If the particles are grouped in bunches, then we see a pulse of energy each time a group sweeps by. This is the source of the pulses. The faster the star spins, the more pulses we see per second. See Figure 3.

The February 1989 flashes detected from Sanduleak have one very unusual feature: They occur at a rate of about two

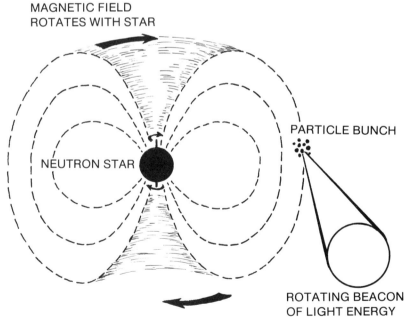

MAGNETIC FIELD
ROTATES WITH STAR

NEUTRON STAR

PARTICLE BUNCH

ROTATING BEACON
OF LIGHT ENERGY

fig. 3

thousand times per second—much faster than theory predicts. This means that at its equator Sanduleak is moving at more than one-third the speed of light. Conventional theory predicts that at such a high speed Sanduleak would fly apart.

One possible explanation is that Sanduleak is emitting not just one but two beams of light, so that its revolution rate is only one thousand revolutions per second—a high rotation rate but not high enough to cause the star to come apart. But this explanation is not without problems. If there were two beams of light, we would not expect them to be identical because they would be coming from different regions of the star. But observations show that the two flashes are identical. So astronomers are still scratching their heads.

We have examined the life history of a relatively massive star. As we have seen, observations across the electromagnetic spectrum have allowed us to follow the star's evolution in some detail as well as to make cross-checks between theory and observation. Part of our story, however, involved observations outside the electromagnetic spectrum—the tiny, almost shadowy particles called neutrinos. Next we shall continue our story of the neutrino as well as some other particles that bring news to Earth of the ever unfolding story of the cosmos.

A New Set
of Building Blocks

Until late in the 1950s, it appeared that all the matter in the universe was fashioned from three basic building blocks—electrons, protons, and neutrons. As nearly as anyone could tell, all the elements from hydrogen to gold to uranium were various configurations of these three ingredients. But then scientists began to detect peculiar particles whose origins were connected with other particles coming from outer space—particles called cosmic rays. These high-energy "rays" smashed into the atoms and molecules in the atmosphere, creating particles that no one had ever observed before.

Cosmic rays were discovered in 1912 by an Austrian physicist, Victor Franz Hess, during an ascent in a balloon. The balloon was equipped with an instrument that had been used primarily to study the strength of X rays and gamma rays—rays created in profusion by radioactive elements like uranium. Hess discovered that the higher his balloon went, the more strongly his instrument reacted. Since there was no uranium or other radioactive substance in the atmosphere—at least not in the amount indicated by his instrument—he concluded that he was measuring some new kind of ray. Because his cosmic rays grew stronger as his balloon rose higher, he believed that they must come from outer space. He reasoned that the rays were weakened as they passed through Earth's atmosphere, and that since there was less atmosphere as he went higher, the rays should be stronger and stronger.

Victor Franz
Hess discovered
cosmic rays
in 1912.

When cosmic rays were first discovered, they were believed to be rays, as their name suggests. That is, they were thought to be some kind of electromagnetic radiation like gamma rays. Gamma rays, we recall, are at the extremely energetic end of the electromagnetic spectrum. Since cosmic rays are extremely energetic, it was natural to associate them with the gamma rays. Further investigation showed, however, that these "cosmic rays" were not rays at all, but charged particles—mostly electrons and protons; and they carry as much energy to Earth as do all of the electromagnetic radiation sources from radio waves to gamma rays, from all of the stars, except the sun. Cosmic particles would be a more appropriate name for them, but the name cosmic rays has stuck even though we know these charged particles are not rays.

Most of the world's physicists were skeptical that the radiation from cosmic rays was coming from outer space. Hess's discovery was not honored with a Nobel prize until twenty-four years after it was first announced. But today we know that cosmic rays exist in great abundance. In fact, about fifty of them have passed through your head since you started reading this sentence.

After studying cosmic rays became a respectable line of research, scientists soon discovered that the intensity of these rays depends on one's location on the surface of Earth. An observer near the north or south pole finds that there are many more cosmic rays per second than an observer making his observations near the equator. This fact was a big clue in determining that cosmic rays are charged particles, not electromagnetic rays.

Any electrically charged particle interacts with a magnetic field, whereas neutral particles pass through magnetic fields as though there were nothing there. Earth has a magnetic field whose north and south poles are roughly aligned with the geographic north and south poles. Charged particles easily travel along the direction of the magnetic field, but they are strongly deflected when they try to travel *across* a magnetic field, as Figure 1 shows.

Cosmic rays traveling from outer space toward Earth's equator are moving roughly across Earth's magnetic field, since this field is parallel to Earth's surface near the equator. On the other hand, the magnetic field is pointing nearly straight up near the

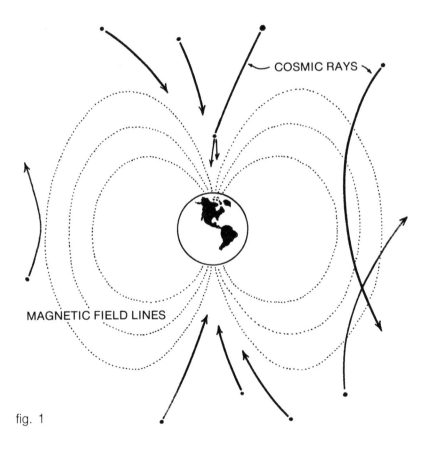

COSMIC RAYS

MAGNETIC FIELD LINES

fig. 1

geographic poles; so the cosmic rays easily make their way to Earth's surface there. At intermediate points between the poles and the equator, cosmic-ray strength has intermediate values, depending on the direction of Earth's magnetic field at the point in question.

One of the great mysteries was—and still is: Where do cosmic rays come from? When an astronomer wants to know where some radiation is coming from, he simply points his telescope toward the radiation and notes the direction in which his telescope is pointed. This procedure works well because electromagnetic radiation travels in straight lines. Starlight doesn't take some circuitous path on its way to Earth; it takes the shortest possible path, a straight line.

But with cosmic rays, because of their electrical charge, an astronomer can't simply point his telescope to find the direction of their source. Cosmic rays, as we've just noted, are deflected by Earth's magnetic field; this alone is enough to confuse the direction of the rays' origin. The problem is compounded by the fact that interstellar space contains gigantic webs of magnetic field; so a cosmic ray on its journey to Earth may have taken a route as circuitous as that of a fly buzzing aimlessly across a room. Nevertheless, there seems to be a slight preponderance of cosmic rays coming from the direction of our Milky Way galaxy, which suggests that it may be the primary source. But the suggestion is controversial.

One reason the early investigators confused cosmic rays with gamma rays was that both have such great energy. There are no particle accelerators on Earth to produce particles that can compete with the energy of cosmic ray particles. Probably there never will be. Many theories have been proposed to account for their high energy, and it is likely that they are energized in more than one way; so several of these theories may be true.

One theory proposes that cosmic rays are batted around in the universe like the ball in a table tennis match. In this case, the batting is done by the interstellar magnetic fields we have mentioned. But this suggestion works only if the fields are moving relative to one another.

As a simple demonstration of how this theory works, let's imagine a table tennis ball bouncing back and forth between two vertical walls. Let's imagine further that the whole process takes place in a vacuum and is free from the pull of gravity. If we neglect the fact that the ball loses a little energy to friction each time it hits a wall, the ball will bounce back and forth between the walls forever, neither gaining nor losing energy.

But suppose that one of the walls is moving toward the other one. When the ball strikes the moving wall, it bounces back with greater speed than it does from the fixed wall. So each time the ball strikes the moving wall, it gains a little energy. As long as the moving wall continues to move toward the ball, the ball continues to gain energy. Eventually it will have enough energy to break through a weak place in one of the walls and escape.

The process is the same with the cosmic ray particles bouncing around in a tangle of interstellar magnetic fields. Each time it meets such a tangle moving toward it, it gains energy. If it bounces off such an approaching magnetic field enough times, it will eventually break through a weak place in the field and start its journey to Earth.

Supernovas are another likely source of cosmic rays. Here the evidence is indirect. As we know, supernovas produce strong bursts of electromagnetic radiation, including gamma rays. The suggestion is that these gamma rays are produced, in part, by cosmic rays created during the star's collapse as the cosmic rays collide with the expanding-gas shell surrounding the collapsed star. This process will produce more gamma rays than we would expect if there were no collisions between the cosmic rays and the expanding-gas shell. Observations indicate that this is indeed the case; excesses of gamma rays are found in light from exploding supernovas. One big advantage of these observations is that the gamma rays, being electromagnetic radiation, travel directly to Earth. So the direction of their arrival suggests the location where the cosmic rays were generated.

Another possible way that cosmic rays may be generated has to do with the fact that they are electrically charged. In this case, however, they are energized not by magnetic fields but by strong electric fields. The process is rather straightforward. A cosmic ray finding itself in an electric field is simply accelerated in the direction of the electric field.

The question then is, Where do the electric fields come from? One answer is pulsars. As we know, pulsars are rapidly spinning neutron stars sweeping strong magnetic fields through space as they rotate. This rotating action can act like a gigantic dynamo, producing electric fields as strong as 100 trillion volts per centimeter at the surface of the pulsar. Such electric fields would directly accelerate charged particles to cosmic ray energies.

In such a process, the energy of the rotating pulsar is slowly but surely carried away by the cosmic rays. This means that pulsars should slow down in their rotation rate as time goes on. This slowing has in fact been observed, but the process comes up short in explaining the number and energies of the observed flux of cosmic rays striking Earth. So we must look for additional sources of cosmic rays.

Another possible source has to do with the binary star systems we have discussed. As we recall, mass from one star flows into the other, creating strong X rays in the process.

In 1972, one of these X-ray binary stars flared up to become one of the strongest emitters of radio waves in the sky. The radio signals suggested that a huge cloud of energetic electrons tangled in a strong magnetic field had been propelled into the space surrounding the two circling stars. Accelerating electrons generate radio waves. So as this giant bubble of electrons and magnetic field expanded, the accelerating electrons spiraling around the magnetic field sapped the bubble of its energy and formed the observed strong radio emissions.

About ten years after these emissions were detected, this same X-ray binary system spewed out jets of particles that moved in opposite directions at speeds up to one-third the speed of light. Such energetic phenomena are strong indicators that here might be the spawning ground for the creation of cosmic rays.

When they enter Earth's atmosphere, most cosmic rays collide with other particles and create a shower of "secondary" cosmic rays. By chance, however, some cosmic rays reach Earth without hitting any of the atoms or molecules that make up our atmosphere. These uncontaminated "primary" cosmic rays are our only direct sample of material from outside our own solar system. Although the sample is not large—perhaps two pounds of material falls on Earth per year—it may be extremely significant.

Our solar system was formed about 4.5 billion years ago, so it represents the material that was prevalent in our part of the universe at that time. Cosmic rays, however, seem to be born continually; so they represent universe material that is much younger. Thus studying the composition of cosmic rays may give a better clue to the present makeup of interstellar space than the material making up our own solar system can give.

A number of scientists have recommended that high priority be given to studying the composition of these primary cosmic rays as a way of learning more about the makeup of the present-day universe. But making such studies requires that cosmic ray detectors be put into probes or satellites above Earth's atmosphere—an expensive undertaking that must compete with all the other projects that scientists with many diverse ideas have in mind.

It is ironic that, although cosmic rays discovered in 1912 provided our first window into the universe outside the visible spectrum, they are the last to be recognized as a valuable tool in our attempts to unravel the nature of the universe. But perhaps in the years ahead, cosmic ray astronomy will take its place alongside radio, visible, infrared, ultraviolet, and gamma-ray astronomy.

Cosmic rays were not the only phenomena that challenged the old theory of just three simple building blocks as the basis for all matter. Other puzzles also appeared. One of the cardinal principles of physics is that energy is always conserved. But now scientists found nuclear reactions in which some of the energy seemed to disappear. If they counted up all the energy carried by the various particles going into a nuclear reaction, and counted up all the energy of the particles released in the same nuclear reaction, some energy was missing.

One suggestion was that some unknown, undetected particle carried off the missing energy. Physicists believed so strongly in the principle of the conservation of energy that they were convinced that such a particle must exist. But it was twenty years after the particle was first proposed that it was finally found, as a byproduct from the reactor cores of nuclear power stations.

The particle was the neutrino, the elusive particle born out of the collapse of stars.

As we have observed, however, catching a neutrino is not easy. The average neutrino could pass unperturbed through a wall of lead 3,500 light-years thick. But the fact that neutrinos have such penetrating power means that they are probably the only way we will ever have of looking into the very heart of stars. In fact, we have already had a look into the supernova of 1987 via the tiny thimbleful of neutrinos detected in the United States and Japan.

Neutrinos also allow us to look into the very center of our closest star, the sun, in a way that not even the strongest gamma-ray emission can. The conversion of hydrogen to helium in our sun gives off both gamma rays and neutrinos. It may take a typical gamma ray as long as a million years to find its way to the sun's surface as the ray collides and interacts with almost every particle it meets along the way. But a neutrino emerges from the sun in seconds.

One uncertainty about the neutrino is whether it has a mass or not. Is it like a bucket of pure energy—a *photon*—of electromagnetic radiation that is massless? Or is it something like a cosmic ray particle with mass? One thing that is known with certainty is that if a neutrino does have mass, the mass is exceedingly small—less than one ten-thousandth the mass of the electron.

From Einstein's theory of relativity we know that only particles that are massless—like photons of light—can travel with the speed of light. So if a neutrino is massless, it can travel with the speed of light; if it has mass, it cannot. Today's standard theory says that neutrinos are massless, but some controversial measurements seem to indicate otherwise.

Some time ago it was suggested that observations from a

nearby supernova might resolve the question. The idea was this: As we know, when the star collapses, electrons in the core of the star are crushed into the atomic nuclei to form neutrons. Neutrinos are emitted in this process. The shock wave created during the collapse of the star creates neutrinos. Assuming that all neutrinos were emitted at the same time, if neutrinos have mass then those with more energy will travel at higher speeds and reach Earth first. But if neutrinos have no mass, then, still assuming that they were all emitted at the same time, they will all arrive at Earth at the same time. Thus, so the theory goes, the spread in arrival time of the neutrinos from a supernova, along with measurements of their energies, should reveal the neutrino's mass, if any.

So what happened when the supernova appeared in February 1987? The measurements in the United States and Japan showed that the neutrinos did not all arrive at the same time. This leaves us with the question of whether the neutrinos have mass and thus arrived at different times because of their different energies, or alternatively, the assumption that all neutrinos were emitted at the same time is not true. That is, in the latter case, the neutrinos may be massless and still arrive at different times simply because they were emitted at different times. So the results are ambiguous; the question of the mass of the neutrino is still undecided. Most neutrino experts believe that supernova events can give only an upper limit to the mass of the neutrino.

Does the answer really matter? As we shall see in the final chapter, the mass of the neutrino, or its lack of mass, may very well decide the ultimate fate of the universe.

With the development of giant particle accelerators, popularly known as atom smashers, scientists discovered even more particles. It became evident that a drastic revision was needed in our understanding of the basic composition of the universe. In the last decade or so, scientists have made great progress in their search for a new set of building blocks. It appears now that all of the basic particles fall into two broad categories—*fermions* and *bosons*. Fermions are the particles that make up matter, and bosons are the particles that carry the forces between the particles of matter. Today there appear to be only four basic forces: gravitational, electromagnetic, *strong nuclear force*, and a fourth called the *weak nuclear force*. All of these forces are associated with various kinds of bosons.

Fermions, the particles that make up matter, are divided into two subgroups: the *quarks* and the *leptons*. It appears that all of the matter in the universe is composed of six different kinds of quarks and six different kinds of leptons. Protons and neutrons, for example, are composed of quarks. The six leptons consist of three sets of twin particles that occur naturally together. The first pair of twins is the electron and the neutrino. The second pair is a kind of heavy, fat electron with a different companion neutrino; and the third pair is an even fatter, heavier electron, also with another, different companion neutrino. So we have three kinds of electrons and three kinds of neutrinos. See Figure 2.

None of these particles are visible, of course, even with the help of the most powerful microscope. Rather, like phenomena beyond the visible ranges in the Planck curve—those in the infrared and ultraviolet and higher regions—scientists must study these particles by their behavior, using atom smashers. They send packets of certain chosen atoms at tremendous speeds through long tunnels wrapped in magnetic fields. By crashing them into other particles, they break the atoms down into particles that they can study.

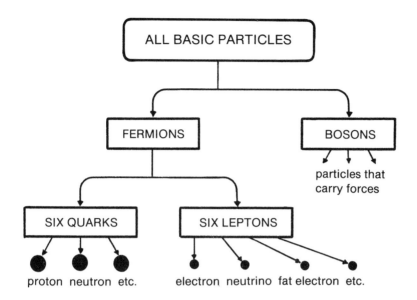

fig. 2

With these twelve particles we can build not only protons and neutrons, but all of the strange particles discovered with atom smashers and associated with cosmic rays. The present theories of bosons and fermions do not limit the number of basic particles. According to these theories, there could be more than twelve. But as we shall see in the final chapter, observations of the structure of the universe may set the number at or near twelve.

10

Neptune's Frosty Pink-and-Blue Moon

We have seen how a remarkable array of telescopes collected electromagnetic and particle emissions from the most distant stars. Such instruments have made visible many things that had been invisible and therefore unknown. Analysis of these emissions has provided us with an understanding of, and appreciation for, the universe that no astronomer a hundred years ago would have dreamed possible. But what of our own backyard, our solar system with its nine planets, numerous comets, asteroids, and dozens of moons circling outlying planets, as well as our own moon?

Certainly earthbound observations of the planets and their companions have given us significant information about our solar system. The same kinds of instruments, from radio to infrared telescopes, have been used with sometimes startling results. Franklin and Burke's fortuitous discovery of radio emissions from Jupiter is a prime example. But the real improvement in our understanding of our solar system has come in much the same way that early explorers on Earth learned of unknown seas, continents, and peoples—by going to look.

Since Russia's launching of *Sputnik* in the 1950s, we have landed exploratory probes on Venus and Mars, set foot on the moon, and propelled spacecraft through the atmospheres of Jupiter, Saturn, Uranus, and Neptune—taking pictures all the time. For these explorations we have not needed to depend on sometimes complex, often brilliant interpretations of our observations. Instead, via our space probe "eyes," we have gone to see for ourselves.

Exploration of the solar system has been one of the most extraordinary successes of the space age. Altogether, Russia and the United States have launched more than seventy-five successful exploratory missions, including the six *Apollo* voyages from 1969 through 1972 that landed American astronauts on the moon.

Solar system exploration falls roughly into three historical eras: before the telescope was invented, the great age of optical telescopes, and now the age of direct planetary exploration.

The first clue that the universe was not the static, unchanging vault in the sky that the Greeks imagined came when Galileo Galilei pointed his telescope toward the sun, the moon, and the planets. Galileo had heard that the Dutch had invented a "magnifying tube" that brought faraway objects near. The discovery of the principle of the telescope was probably an accident. By Galileo's time, spectacles for both farsightedness and nearsightedness were common. Nearsightedness was treated with concave lenses, and farsightedness with convex lenses. An experimenter need only pick up one of each, hold one at arm's length from the other, and peer through the two together to make a telescope.

Galileo discovered
that the moon had
mountains similar to
the mountains on Earth.

When Galileo heard of the Dutch discovery, he headed for his nearest optician's shop, and within an hour or so had constructed a telescope from a hollow tube and two spectacle lenses. These first simple telescopes had a magnifying power of about three. Galileo quickly improved the original Dutch version, producing telescopes with powers up to thirty times. That is, they made objects three hundred feet away, for example, appear to be only ten feet away, and showed details that could be seen if one were only ten feet from the object.

As far as we know, Galileo was the first to point a telescope toward the heavens. Why the Dutch had not done this we do not know. Some have suggested that exploring and wondering about the heavens was not condoned by the church. But Galileo, who challenged many popular beliefs with his scientific experiments and measurements, was not deterred by such a notion.

Galileo quickly discovered that the moon had mountains that

he likened to the mountains on Earth. He could see the moving line between night and day on the moon as tall mountain shadows shrank and disappeared when the sun moved over them. What his telescope could not show him—as no optical telescope can—was the back side of the moon. Because of the mutual gravitational interaction between Earth and the moon, the moon always keeps the same face toward Earth. So it was not until the early days of the space age that we got our first view of the back side of the moon. A Russian space probe collected the first pictures, and later the *Apollo* astronauts obtained more detailed pictures. The pictures revealed that the moon's back side is far more cratered and at a higher average elevation than the familiar front side, which is covered with large flat areas first seen in detail by Galileo and called *maria*, the Latin word for "seas."

With his telescope Galileo also discovered that the sun had spots that moved along with its rotation. And when he pointed his telescope toward Jupiter, he saw what at first he thought were four faint stars in the plane of Jupiter's equator. But much to his astonishment, a few days later the stars had moved. In his characteristic meticulous manner, Galileo carefully plotted the positions of the "stars" from day to day. Soon he realized that they were not stars but moons of Jupiter, like Earth's moon. He named them, in order of their distance from Jupiter, Io, Europa, Ganymede, and Callisto, after lovers and companions of the Greek god Zeus, the Roman Jupiter. Collectively Galileo called the four moons the Medicean Stars, in the hope that honoring the Medicis, the famous Italian ruling family, would influence wealthy Florentine patrons to support his work.

In this brief space we cannot examine adequately the many advances that dozens of space probes have brought to our understanding of the solar system. Instead we shall focus on what we have learned about two of the Medicean Stars and one of the moons of Uranus, a planet unknown to Galileo. This small sample of recent probes will reveal the wondrous results that planetary exploration has achieved in the last few years.

In March 1972, the spacecraft *Pioneer 10* was launched from the Kennedy Space Center. It reached Jupiter about a year later. "Manning" and maneuvering the many pieces of scientific equipment aboard the spacecraft was an uncommon feat that required something like ten thousand commands during the approach to Jupiter. And because of Jupiter's distance from Earth, the control signals from the Jet Propulsion Laboratories in California took forty-five minutes to get to the spacecraft, traveling at the speed of light.

Pioneer 10 provided us with our first really good look at Jupiter, via television signals broadcast back to Earth. And what a view it was! The picture unveiled alternating dark and bright bands of light running parallel to Jupiter's equator. The bands were shades of red, yellow, orange, and blue. And in Jupiter's southern hemisphere lay the famous Giant Red Spot, a reddish oval of swirling, turbulent gases. Early astronomers had thought the red spot might be some enormous dust storm, or perhaps even fumes from a volcano. Probably the spot represents a gigantic storm, about the size of Earth, sometimes even three or four times Earth's size, that has persisted for at least three hundred years.

Infrared detectors aboard *Pioneer 10* revealed that Jupiter radiated almost twice as much energy as it received from the sun. It was clear, then, that Jupiter is more than just an inert, gigantic, spherical mass of compressed hydrogen and other gases. Some astronomers have suggested that it is more like a failed sun than a planet. Its mass is more than three hundred times that of Earth, and its diameter is more than ten times as great. Thus Jupiter is near the critical mass at which it could

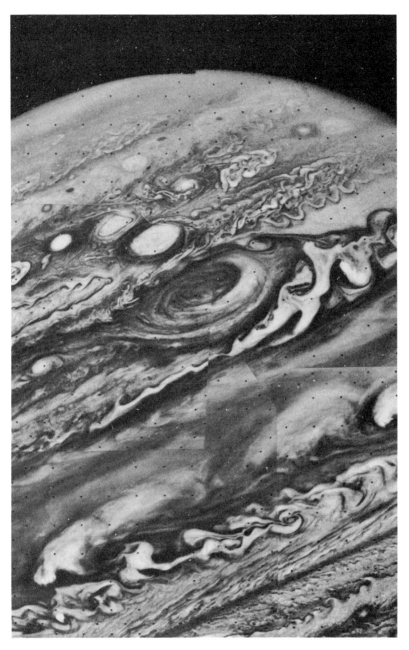

Jupiter's red spot is probably a gigantic storm that has persisted for at least three hundred years.

undergo enough gravitational collapse to start a nuclear furnace in its core. In fact, some Russian scientists have proposed such a possibility for Jupiter's future.

Pioneer 10 also mapped out Jupiter's magnetic field. This field, more than nineteen thousand times as strong as Earth's magnetic field, is swept around rapidly once in every ten hours, the length of Jupiter's day. Because of the radio emissions discovered by Franklin and Burke, scientists suspected much earlier that such fields might exist. The most likely explanation of the radio signals was that they were produced by electrons spiraling around and along very strong magnetic field lines.

The magnetic field is a product of both Jupiter's rapid rotation rate and enormous pressure at its core. The hydrogen gas, under such extreme conditions, breaks down into its component parts, protons and electrons. And just as a current of electrons flowing through a copper wire creates a magnetic field around the wire, so the electrons rotating with Jupiter create gigantic magnetic fields.

After reporting on Jupiter, *Pioneer 10* sped on beyond the border of the known solar system. Guaranteed for only twenty-one months when it was launched, the spacecraft is now close to twenty years old. It has traveled four billion miles and is still sending its messages back to Earth as it searches for a mysterious Planet X that some scientists believe may be orbiting the sun beyond Pluto.

A later flight to Jupiter by the spacecraft *Voyager I* cast "shocking" light on Jupiter's magnetic field. *Voyager I* took many close-up views of Jupiter's moons, especially the innermost moon, Io. Io rotates around Jupiter about once every two days, while Jupiter itself revolves once every ten hours. This means that Io, because of its proximity to Jupiter, has a strong, rapidly moving magnetic field passing through it continuously.

Io is Jupiter's innermost moon.

This sets up an enormous electrical charge on Io, which discharges from time to time in what must be the most colossal lightning flash ever detected by man. The bolt travels more than 240,000 miles on its way to Jupiter, creating a burst of radio static that can be heard half a billion miles away by ordinary shortwave receivers on Earth.

Another spacecraft, *Voyager II*, arrived at Jupiter's doorstep in July 1979 after a journey of almost two years. *Voyager II*, which like *Pioneer 10* is still functioning, is truly a tribute to man's ingenuity. Most spacecraft operating nearer the sun depend on the sun's rays to supply their electric power needs. But the sun's feeble rays at Jupiter's great distance cannot meet these needs. So a small, onboard nuclear power plant fueled by radioactive pellets of plutonium supplies several hundred watts of power.

The spacecraft itself is a marvel of redundancy. If one system fails another is there to back it up. Considering that there are millions of parts in the spacecraft, which weighs nearly a ton and would fill a good-sized living room, this is a remarkable achievement.

Three computers keep track of the health of the spacecraft and perform scientific functions. *Voyager II* carries a variety of devices to make infrared, ultraviolet, and radio measurements, as well as other devices to detect magnetic fields and charged particles. But the most productive results have been obtained from the two on-board television cameras, which have relayed pictures back to Earth even more spectacular than those obtained by the *Pioneer 10* probe.

On July 9, 1979, *Voyager II* sent back pictures of Europa, the moon second closest to Jupiter. Although it is about the size of our moon, Europa's surface proved to be entirely different. Europa resembled a shiny, smooth billiard ball with numerous cracks and blemishes. Measurements suggested that the shiny surface was a layer of ice, perhaps sixty miles thick. The cracks and blemishes were probably due to meteorites that had smashed into Europa, cracking and cratering its surface.

Even more bizarre than the sight of Europa was the view of Io, Jupiter's closest moon. Io is also about the size of our moon and is probably the reddest object in our solar system—redder even than the red planet Mars. Pictures showed that Io's orbit around Jupiter was a great doughnut shape stuffed with atoms of sulfur, sodium, and potassium—material somehow strewn about and left by Io as it circled Jupiter. As pictures came in, scientists at the Jet Propulsion Laboratories jokingly referred to Io as a pizza or a spoiled orange.

Another astonishing revelation was that Io was covered with volcanoes spewing out material that sprayed 120 miles high. During a routine inspection of the *Voyager II* transmissions, Linda Morabito, a *Voyager* navigation specialist, was amazed when she saw a large bubble-shaped cloud erupt from one of Io's

Europa resembles a shiny, smooth billiard ball with numerous cracks and blemishes.

volcanoes. She was the very first person ever to see an active volcano not on Earth.

Altogether nine volcanoes were discovered spewing out large amounts of molten sulfur and continually reshaping Io's surface. No wonder Io looked like a spoiled orange! And the maps of Io are good only for a few months.

About a week before the first Io pictures reached Earth, a prophetic scientific paper appeared; prepared by several American scientists, it predicted that active volcanoes would be found on Io. But these volcanoes are not due to a molten interior core occasionally breaking through the surface—like the volcanoes here on Earth. The energy driving Io's volcanoes comes from the continuous battering it undergoes by the forces of Jupiter's gravity on one side and the forces of gravity of Jupiter's moons beyond Io's orbit. These two sets of forces, constantly tugging Io in opposite directions, churn its interior and develop the equivalent of more than two thousand tons of TNT exploding every second. Much of this energy finds its way to Io's surface

Linda Morabito
was the first
person to see
a volcano erupt
in outer space.

This eruption on the dark (right) rim of Io looks like a large bubble-shaped cloud.

as volcanic explosions. Doubtless it is these explosions that fill Io's surrounding doughnut with material.

After exploring Jupiter and its moons, *Voyager II* journeyed on to Saturn, where it took equally spectacular pictures. Nobody had expected the spaceship's electronic equipment to survive more than five years. But when it became apparent that *Voyager II* would likely be in working order as it passed Uranus, the scientists were overjoyed.

Uranus, the seventh planet from the sun, was discovered with a homemade telescope by the English astronomer William Herschel in 1781. But compared to information that had been gathered about planets closer to Earth, little was known about Uranus. Still, a few facts had been established: Uranus took eighty-four years to circle the sun. It had five moons along with nine spider-web-thin rings made up of blackish particles. It was about seventeen times as massive as Earth, and its greenish blue color was probably due to an atmosphere of mostly hydrogen and helium surrounding a deep ocean consisting of melted ice water and ammonia and methane. What was not known, among other things, was the length of its day. *Voyager II* scientists hoped to discover answers.

A troublesome problem of the extended journey had to do with how the TV pictures were sent back to Earth. *Voyager II*'s computers had been programmed to process and return photos only from Jupiter and Saturn, not from the exceedingly dim terrain of Uranus. Computer experts back on Earth rewrote the necessary computer programs and then radioed them to *Voyager II*, replacing the old programs. Then on January 24, 1986, the spaceship arrived at Uranus. It was precisely one minute and nine seconds ahead of the time scheduled some eight years earlier, when *Voyager II* was launched in August 1977. It had traveled almost two billion miles.

As *Voyager II* approached Uranus, the prospects for gaining new knowledge seemed poor. All that appeared at first was Uranus's blue-green surface; there was no evidence of radio emissions, and no magnetic field. It looked as if Uranus, unlike the spectacular Jupiter, might turn out to be the dud planet of our solar system.

But that prospect was soon to change. As *Voyager II* closed in on Uranus, radio emissions were detected, and a magnetic field about as strong as that of Earth was found. Ten tiny moons, too small to be seen from Earth, were spotted in the images relayed back to Earth, along with another ring that had never been seen before, bringing the total to ten rings. Rapidly moving high-altitude clouds in the Uranian atmosphere revealed that winds exceeding 200 miles an hour were whipping up its atmosphere.

During *Voyager II*'s nearly three-hour flyby of Uranus, some 7,000 images made by the TV cameras took two hours and forty-five minutes to arrive on Earth. It was another triumph for the Voyager program.

Uranus's radio emissions proved to be the key to determining the length of its day. As the solar wind from the sun streams by Uranus, it interacts with the radio emissions rotating in step with Uranus. This creates a pattern of radio emissions that repeats itself once every seventeen hours, thus revealing the length of Uranus's day.

But the most spectacular observation was yet to come. As good fortune would have it, *Voyager II* passed nearest of all to Miranda, one of the moons of Uranus. Miranda, about 300 miles in diameter, was discovered in 1948. It is the closest of Uranus's moons and is probably composed largely of ice and chunks of rock. It gave every indication of being one of the more boring hunks of real estate in the universe. But as it turned out, it is one of the most bizarre geological objects ever observed by man.

One planetary geologist wrote his observations of it: "We are still trying to invent words to describe this place. . . . Parts [of Miranda] have been ripped and shredded into great faults, cliffs, canyons, and ridges. One area looks like a huge jagged crystal. Two rectangular areas have ridges that could have been carved by a giant plough or rake. They curve almost at right angles. Some of the cliffs are three miles in height. Another area . . . looks like layers of pancakes."

An overall view of Miranda roughly resembles a slightly squashed potato. How could such a monstrous object ever have come about? The answer seems to be that Miranda was struck by a meteor or some other object that smashed it to pieces. The collision wasn't hard enough, though, to scatter the pieces beyond the reach of gravity. Like the broken parts of Humpty-Dumpty lying together at the foot of the wall, Miranda's parts probably lay scattered in a narrow ring, finally reassembling themselves under their mutual gravitational attraction into a new version of Miranda. As the pieces came together, the rocky parts sank toward Miranda's middle, while the lighter, icy parts moved to the surface. The sinking rocks created hot spots, which accounted at least in part for Miranda's grotesque surface.

On more detailed inspection it appears that Miranda has been broken apart—probably by collisions with meteorlike objects— and reassembled by the force of gravity a number of times. Thus this Humpty-Dumpty moon has not only been put back together again, but has been put back together again several times.

Uranus's Humpty-Dumpty moon was not the end of the *Voyager II* story. On August 24, 1989, the aging spacecraft, beginning the thirteenth year of its journey and 2.75 billion miles from Earth, passed within 3,048 miles of the planet Neptune. *Voyager*'s TV cameras, whose images took more than four hours to reach Earth at the speed of light, revealed blue-topped clouds, six moons never known before, a magnetic field tilted at 50 degrees to Neptune's axis of rotation, and at least five rings circling the planet.

Several days earlier, scientists watching the approach to Neptune had observed a gigantic blue spot large enough to engulf Earth. More detailed photos revealed that the giant spot is a huge storm, similar to Jupiter's red spot, with winds exceeding 700 miles per hour. These observations greatly puzzle scientists because the sun at Neptune's distance from it is only one-thousandth as bright as it is on Earth. So unlike Earth, where the sun provides enough energy to fuel our weather, Neptune cannot receive nearly enough solar energy to explain its weather. One suggestion is that the energy comes from heat generated somewhere inside the planet. But estimates of this energy do not seem large enough to account for Neptune's violent atmosphere.

A few hours after its closest approach to Neptune, *Voyager* passed within 23,888 miles of Neptune's largest moon, Triton. The images of Triton, which is about the size of Earth's moon, turned out to be totally unexpected. The moon's icy pink-and-blue surface is pocked with craters created by collisions with meteors. One observer said Triton's surface looked like the veined skin of a cantaloupe. Most surprising, Triton, long thought to be a totally dead moon, is apparently dotted with active volcanoes—volcanoes scientists say probably explain the curious black marks on the moon's surface. So Triton, like Jupiter's Io, may join Earth as one of only three bodies in our solar system to have active volcanoes.

Overall, Triton is a white sphere with a pinkish, sometimes bluish cast. At 400 degrees below zero Fahrenheit, it is the coldest object ever observed in the solar system. The pink color is probably due to radiation damage to the methane ice. Ice crystals of nitrogen, methane, and carbon monoxide are clear, but appear to be blue in certain lights.

It will be years before scientists are able to digest completely the masses of information relayed back to Earth by *Voyager II* on its Grand Tour of our solar system. But the Grand Tour is not yet over. Scientists estimate that *Voyager II* has enough fuel to keep it going for another twenty-five years. By then it will be 130 times as far from the sun as Earth is, and it will probably have crossed the boundary between the realm ruled by the sun and what scientists call the "interstellar medium." The solar realm ends where the sun's solar wind becomes so weak that it is overcome by the stellar winds of other stars. This boundary crossing will occur around the year 2012—about the time when *Voyager*'s signals will become too faint to detect on Earth.

In about 6,500 years, *Voyager*, coasting on its momentum, will come near its first star since leaving our solar system, Bernard's Star. Then, in another 11,500 years, it will approach the star Proxima Centauri. By 26,262, *Voyager* will enter the Oort cloud, the cloud believed to be the birthplace of comets. And then it will drift on toward the Dog Star, Sirius, the brightest star visible from Earth, making its closest approach in the year 296,036.

If some intelligent beings should make contact with *Voyager II* before that time—or after—they will find, mounted on the spaceship's exterior, a phonograph record of sounds from Earth—music from Bach and Beethoven, and voices speaking more than a hundred different languages.

11

The Mystery
of the Missing Mass

In Chapter 1 we considered Olbers' paradox of why the sky is not bright both night and day. We considered some possible solutions—that starlight is absorbed by some intervening material in interstellar space, for example—and found all such solutions wanting in one way or another. We also hinted that Edgar Allen Poe had come near the correct solution in his poem "Eureka." Now we shall take up Olbers' paradox again and look at it in the light of what we know today about the cosmos.

Man has always been perplexed about the origin of the universe. The view after Newton was that the universe was static and had existed forever. This does away with the problem of origins but brings up the equally perplexing problem of how something could have existed forever and have infinite extent. It was this belief, we recall, that led to Olbers' paradox.

But as we have learned in the last few chapters, the universe is anything but static. Stars do not last forever; they come and go, sometimes bowing out with a spectacular last performance.

Here, then, is the missing part of the key to unlocking Olbers' paradox.

The other two parts we already know. One was Roemer's measurements of Jupiter's moons, which revealed that light travels with a very high but finite speed. The other is the idea of the lookout distance. This, we recall, is the greatest distance we can see, because objects beyond the lookout distance are obscured at that distance or closer by other objects in the way. If we consider the size of the average star, the lookout distance in the universe turns out to be about 100 billion trillion light-years.

Let's put these parts together to resolve Olbers' paradox. Consider a typical star at the lookout distance. During its life of some ten billion years, it emits a beam of light ten billion light-years long—considerably shorter than the 100 billion trillion light-years this "spear" of light must travel to reach us. Other typical closer stars will also generate spears of light ten billion light-years long. These spears reach us at different times, depending on the distance between us and their launching points. Thus Earth is bathed in a steady stream of spears of light of finite duration, not the accumulated "pileup" of light from stars that have lasted forever. Accordingly, the energy of starlight illuminating Earth is very much less than the light that would have been generated by the assumptions that led to Olbers' paradox.

How much less? We can use Einstein's famous equation $E = MC^2$ to find an answer. E is energy, M is mass, and C is the speed of light. The equation, which is the basis for atomic bombs and power plants, says that mass can be converted into energy. With this equation, plus our knowledge of the amount of mass in the universe, we can estimate the maximum light that all the stars and all the rest of the objects in space could possibly generate on Earth—or any other place in the universe, for that matter. And we must remember that *light* means the whole electromagnetic spectrum, from radio waves to gamma rays.

The way we get our answer is a good example of what physicists call a back-of-the-envelope calculation. Such calculations give us an easy-to-obtain, ballpark estimate of what to expect without going into long, laborious considerations.

If we took all of the atoms in the universe—those in stars, planets, interstellar space, and whatever other material objects may be in space—and spread them uniformly throughout the universe, we would find a density of matter that amounts to about one hydrogen atom per cubic yard. Not very much.

Now suppose that all the mass in each of these atoms were converted into pure radiant energy. What temperature in space would all this energy amount to? That is, what would be the temperature of each cubic meter of space as a result of the energy generated by this one hydrogen atom, according to Einstein's equation?

The temperature is incredibly low—far below the temperature at which hydrogen turns into liquid. It turns out to be about 20 degrees above absolute zero on the Kelvin temperature scale. To give some feel for the Kelvin scale, water freezes at 273 degrees on this scale and boils at 373 degrees. So we see that 20 degrees above zero is very, very cold indeed.

How much light would illuminate Earth under these conditions? No light at all—at least not any that we could see. A blackbody at 20 degrees Kelvin radiates most of its energy in the radio part of the spectrum, and the amount it would radiate in the visible part of the spectrum is so small that we know of no instrument that could detect it.

Rechecking our back-of-the-envelope calculation, we need to

point out that it is too generous in the amount of energy it suggests would be created in the actual case. As we have seen, only a small portion of the mass of a star turns into energy during its lifetime. Most of the mass ends up as a cooling cinder in space. So in the real case, when all of the stars in the universe have at last radiated their final spears of light into space, the universe will be very much colder than we calculated.

Or will it? As we shall see shortly, the answer may depend crucially on a question we raised earlier—Does the neutrino have mass?

We said that the lookout distance in the universe is about 100 billion trillion light-years. This distance comes about purely because of the average size of the average star. The question then is: Are there stars beyond the lookout distance? Or putting the question differently: What is the size of the universe? Is it larger or smaller than the lookout distance?

Newton's answer was that the universe was larger than the lookout distance. Much larger. Infinite, in fact. But let's see what the astronomical observations of our time tell us about the size of the universe.

The Big Dipper is perhaps the best known constellation in the northern hemisphere. To even our most ancient ancestors, it was a familiar sight. It appeared to them exactly as it does to us. This apparent fixed configuration of stars was the single most important factor that suggested that the universe was static and everlasting. Careful measurements in the early part of the eighteenth century revealed, however, that in fact the stars were moving ever so slightly with respect to one another.

When astronomers measure the motion of a star, they usually think of this motion as having two parts or components. The *radial* component is the part of the motion that is either directly toward us or directly away from us. Of course, no star is likely to be moving directly toward or away from us. It is most likely to be moving in some arbitrary direction. So to specify the motion completely, we need to measure the component of motion that is at right angles to the direction of the radial motion—the *transverse* motion, as Figure 1 shows. Astronomers measure radial and transverse motion in two different ways.

In the early part of the eighteenth century, it was the transverse motion that astronomers measured. They did it by making extremely careful measurements of the location of a star against the background sky. By measuring the position over long periods of time, they could see the star shift its position, if ever so slowly.

Measuring radial motion had to await the discovery of the spectral lines of stars. We recall that these lines are at very particular frequencies corresponding to the allowed jumps of the electrons circling an atom. Let's suppose, however, that the star is moving either away from or toward us at a high rate of speed. If it is moving toward us, all of its spectral lines will appear to be at a higher frequency than if the star were at rest. How much higher depends on how fast the star is moving. The greater the speed toward us, the greater the frequency shift.

Just the opposite is true for a star moving away from us. The shifts are to a lower frequency; and the greater the speed away from us, the greater the shift. Thus by measuring the shift in frequency of a particular spectral line, we can determine the radial speed of a star either toward or away from us. These shifts are called *Doppler shifts*, after their discoverer.

We meet Doppler shifts almost every day. As we listen to the honking horn of an oncoming and then departing car, we hear the pitch of the honking change from low to high and then to low again as the car approaches and then departs. If we measured this change in pitch, we could determine the radial compo-

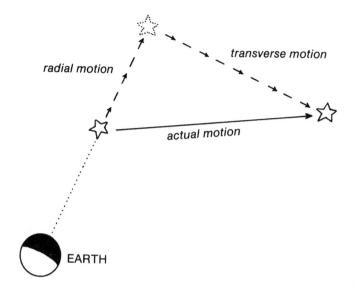

radial motion

transverse motion

actual motion

EARTH

fig. 1

nent of the car's motion. The situation is exactly like measuring the radial component of the motion of a star.

Measuring the Doppler shifts of many stars resulted in a very basic and surprising astronomical discovery by a well-known American astronomer, Edwin Hubble. In 1929 Hubble announced that, on the basis of his studies of Doppler shifts of particular stars in remote clusters of stars akin to our Milky Way galaxy, the universe was expanding. Furthermore, he said, the more distant the star was from us, the faster it moved away from us. One astronomer later described the discovery as "the most astounding fact of the 20th century."

When astronomers first explored the radial motion of the stars via the Doppler-shift measurements, most believed that the stars were moving randomly in all directions; on the average, as many moved toward us as away from us. This was a variation on the Greek idea that the universe was static. That is, although each star moved relative to the others, the net result of all these motions was that the universe, on average, was neither contracting nor expanding, because for every star that moved away from

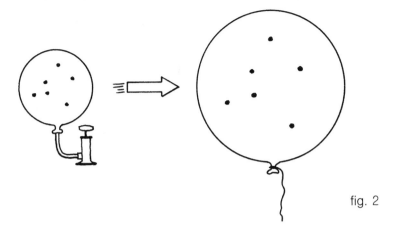

fig. 2

us, another moved toward us. This belief was more a matter of faith that the Greek notion was basically correct than it was a matter of proof by observation.

There were two ways to look at Hubble's discovery. The first was to say that our Milky Way galaxy sat in the middle of the universe and that all other stars moved away from us as circular waves of water expand from the point of impact of a stone thrown into the water. The other was to say that the whole universe was uniformly expanding in all directions, like dots of ink on an expanding balloon. Here each dot moves away from every other dot, as Figure 2 shows, and the greater the distance between any two dots, the greater the speed at which they recede from each other. Since it seemed unlikely that we were at the exact center of the universe, the second explanation was accepted.

When Einstein presented his general theory of relativity in 1916, mathematical astronomers quickly worked out its consequences for the universe. To their astonishment, they found the theory implied that the universe was expanding. But even Einstein, no doubt the most independent scientific thinker of our

Edwin Hubble discovered that the universe is expanding.

age, and probably any other, was so much under the influence of the Greek idea of a static universe that he revised his equations to make the expansion go away. If Einstein had stuck to his guns, he would have made one of the most incredible scientific predictions of all time. As it was, when he heard of Hubble's discovery some thirteen years later, he said that revising his equations had been the biggest blunder of his life.

As more and more mathematically inclined astronomers came to terms with the general theory of relativity, they spun out its implications for the universe in greater and greater detail, and with great delight. What they found was that, although the universe started out expanding, it could collapse later or keep on expanding forever. But there was not enough astronomical evidence to confirm any of these predictions at the time, and evidence is still lacking.

One certain conclusion about an expanding universe is that it can't always have been expanding. If we go back a few million years, the universe would have been smaller than it is now. And if we go back a few billion years, it would have been even smaller—a lot smaller. In fact, if we go back far enough, we finally reach a time when the universe has shrunk to nothing. Based on this kind of argument, that time was about 15 billion years ago—much less than the 100 billion trillion light-years to the lookout distance.

The idea that the universe expanded from nothing to its present size in about 15 billion years seemed so farfetched that most scientists did not think it worth pursuing. But an irreverent, fun-loving, and imaginative scientist from Russia, George Gamow, thought the evidence was so compelling that the idea had to be taken seriously. He started thinking about the consequences of such an idea in the early 1930s.

Today we call Gamow's explanation of an expanding universe

the Big Bang theory—an apt name. In this theory the universe, in the smallest possible instant after its origin, was an incredibly hot, incredibly dense object expanding outwardly at a speed we cannot begin to comprehend. At this early stage, the particles making up the universe were the quarks, leptons, and bosons— the basic particles of matter that we mentioned earlier.

As the universe cooled, the particles came together, making mostly hydrogen and helium atoms. This happened about one million years after the Big Bang, and is an important event called the era of recombination. Recombination refers to the combining of electrons and protons to produce hydrogen and helium. Before the recombination there were so many collisions between buckets of light—photons—and the protons and electrons and other particles that the photons could not escape into space. But after the formation of hydrogen and helium, the photons escaped into space unimpeded. In other words, the photons making up the flash of light associated with the Big Bang were trapped inside the original fireball of protons and electrons; so an observer standing outside this fireball could not have seen anything until about a million years after the Big Bang. This blinding flash of light corresponds to blackbody radiation at a temperature of about 3,000 degrees Kelvin.

But what of that light today? As the universe continued to expand after the era of recombination, the waves of light making up the primordial flash were stretched along with the universe so that today these waves are in the microwave radio region; these wavelengths are much longer than those of the visible region. The radiation has so cooled by this stretching effect that the primordial flash today corresponds to a blackbody temperature of about three degrees above absolute zero on the Kelvin scale. Gamow believed that if the universe was created in a Big Bang, this almost imperceptible cool light must still exist.

At the time, no one took Gamow seriously enough to look for this radiation. It was discovered accidentally in the 1960s, and its two discoverers received a Nobel prize a few years later for their discovery. The temperature Gamow had predicted proved to be very near what was later observed. One of the amazing things about the radiation was that, no matter in which direction scientists looked, they found it remarkably uniform. We shall return to this point shortly.

Before the discovery of Gamow's cool light, thinking seriously about the origin and evolution of the universe was more an exercise for philosophers and theologians than for scientists. But after the discovery, scientific theorizing about the universe became respectable. Today theories of origins have developed to the point that most scientists believe they pretty well understand the evolution of the universe from a tiny fraction of a second after the Big Bang to the present time.

Science has always sought to explain as much of the universe

George Gamow
was the father of the
Big Bang theory
of the origin of
the universe.

as possible using the minimum number of basic laws. We have noted how Maxwell brought together the apparently unrelated laws of magnetism and electricity into a unified electromagnetic theory. Today the search for fewer and more basic laws of nature continues as scientists look for so-called unified theories that we have mentioned before.

One of the most successful of today's unified theories has brought Maxwell's electromagnetic forces together with the weak nuclear force. So we really should say now that there are only three basic forces—the electromagnetic-weak force, the strong nuclear force, and the force of gravity.

More recently another theory, the grand unified theory, has appeared. It brings together the electromagnetic-weak force with the strong nuclear force. Although this theory does not have the kind of experimental verification that the electromagnetic-weak force theory has, it has such theoretical appeal that it is the basis of a new and improved big bang theory—the so-called inflationary theory.

The theory's name comes from its prediction that the universe underwent a dramatic expansion shortly after its birth, and then settled down into the expansion rate we see today. This theory is especially appealing because it explains why the microwave radiation left over from the Big Bang is so uniform in whatever direction we look.

Why do astronomers consider this uniformity a problem? Well, here we are, some 15 billion years after the Big Bang, and we observe that radiation coming from two entirely different directions—from two regions of space that could be as far as 30 billion light-years away from each other—does not differ by more than one-thousandth of 1 percent. Why should two such unrelated parts of the universe emit almost identical radiation?

The inflationary theory provides the answer. According to the theory, very near the moment of the Big Bang all parts of the universe were in intimate contact with each other. So in a sense, the far-flung corners of the universe that are today billions of light-years away are a piece of the same "pie." That is, before inflation, the parts of the universe that are so far from us now were in our neighborhood.

Another important prediction of the inflationary theory is that the universe should be nearly "flat." That is, the distribution of material throughout the universe should be very uniform, on the average, and the density of this material should be very near a particular critical value.

This prediction relates to a subject we brought up earlier. We recall that the general theory of relativity predicts that the universe can keep on expanding forever, or it may eventually collapse on itself. The answer depends on the density and distribution of material in the universe.

Actually, there is a midway possibility in which the distribution and density of mass throughout the universe are just teetering between expansion and contraction. If the density were a little greater than the critical value, the universe would eventually collapse on itself under its own self-gravity. But if the density were just a little less than the critical value, then the universe would not have quite enough mass to be under the control of gravity and would continue to expand.

We can relate this critical density to the density of the universe in the moments after the Big Bang. Observations today indicate that the universe is near the critical density; that is, it is nearly flat. Moments after the Big Bang, the fate of the universe was very dependent on its density. If it had been just the smallest bit *more* dense than the critical density, it would have quickly collapsed on itself into a black hole—and we wouldn't be here.

If, on the other hand, it had been the smallest bit *under* the critical density, it would have mushroomed rapidly and would be wide open and virtually empty today. And, again, we wouldn't be here. In other words, for us to be here requires that the universe be flat, or incredibly close to flat.

How does the inflationary theory bring about this flatness? According to the theory, the universe ballooned outward at a speed greater than the speed of light in less than one millionth of a second, to billions of times its previous size. So the part we see today is only a small part of the total universe and thus appears flat. It's like standing in our backyard and thinking Earth is flat because we see such a small portion of its totality.

We've said that observations indicate that the universe is nearly flat, and thus near its critical density. We need to be a little more specific. The observed density of the universe is about 10 percent of the density required for the critical density, or a little less. This may not seem very close. But consider that the observed density might be millions and billions of times greater or smaller than the critical density; in these terms, the observed value is remarkably near the critical value. So we have a kind of chicken-and-egg problem. The fact that we are here says something about the density of the universe.

In any case, the inflationary theory prediction that the universe is flat is so compelling that astronomers are looking for the missing 90 percent of the mass that would make it flat. This missing 90 percent is the greatest mystery facing astronomers today.

As long as fifty years ago there were strong hints that there was a large part of the universe that we were not seeing. A cluster of stars, the Coma cluster, about 300 million light-years away but relatively near as distances in the universe go, acted very strangely. The stars in the cluster moved around each other in peculiar ways, strongly suggesting that there was some dark, unseen mass that was acting gravitationally on the stars.

Later observations of the Andromeda galaxy, a galaxy much like our own Milky Way galaxy, also hinted at some hidden mass at work. The stars far away from the center of the galaxy circled the center much too fast. The rate at which an object circles a star depends on its distance from the star and the mass of the star. The nearer the object is to the star and the greater the star's mass, the faster the object circles. Similarly, the stars circling the center of the Andromeda galaxy at a certain distance should be circling at a certain rate. But they were circling at a rate much too fast for the measured mass of the center of the Andromeda galaxy. So scientists are faced with the strong possibility that Andromeda has some kind of mass that they haven't been able to observe. And this invisibility includes all of their observations from radio telescopes to gamma-ray telescopes.

Many suggestions have been made to account for the missing mass. One of the most popular is to assume that the neutrino has just enough mass to make up for the missing mass. The problem with this suggestion is that the neutrino is so elusive and energetic that it is hard to understand how the galaxies formed in the way they did under the influence of a very slightly massive neutrino.

Some of the unified theories predict all kinds of exotic subatomic particles, and there is a temptation to attribute the missing mass to them. One problem with most of these theories is that there seems to be no upper limit to the number of particles they predict.

Here some astronomical observations may prove helpful. Since the universe, in its earliest stage, was composed of the most elementary particles—the quarks, leptons, and so on—the constitution of the universe today tells us something about the nature and kinds of elementary particles that make it up. The way our universe looks today suggests that we need at most only five different families of quarks and leptons and their associated particles. So the numerous other particles that some unified theories predict seem not to be a necessary part of our universe, and therefore probably cannot account for the missing mass.

Another suggestion is that the universe contains many Jupiterlike bodies too small and too dim to be seen. And another is that our galaxy, and others like it, contain at their centers massive black holes whose masses equal millions and millions of suns. Although there is some evidence to support this suggestion, the evidence is not conclusive.

One line of investigation relating to the search for black holes and other cataclysmic events in the universe has to do with what are called *gravitational waves*. From Einstein's general theory of relativity, we know that space and time are distorted in the presence of massive bodies like a black hole. If such a body collided with another massive body, or underwent some other kind of cataclysmic eruption, it would launch a ripple in the space-time fabric of the universe that would expand outwardly at the speed of light. Detectors have been set up on Earth to intercept these waves, but to date none has been found conclusively. If one were found, however, it could initiate a whole new branch of astronomy, just as happened with radio astronomy after World War II.

We cannot list here all of the other suggestions for explaining the missing mass. Some have come out of attempts to join all four of the basic forces of matter into what is called a TOE, or theory of everything. But it seems clear that the inflationary theory has such a strong appeal that the astronomical world is going to be very much surprised if somehow, someday, the missing mass doesn't show up.

Epilogue

Before closing we should return to the philosophical question we raised earlier: Is astronomy really a science, since astronomers cannot experiment on the universe?

Not long ago the creator of the inflationary theory, Alan Guth, of the Massachusetts Institute of Technology, made an astounding statement: "Now we have the mathematical tools that allow us to seriously discuss the prospects of creating a universe in our basement."

Guth was smiling slightly, but he was making a serious point. Suppose, Guth proposes, we could somehow create a tiny, compressed region in space whose temperature and pressure resemble the conditions of the Big Bang. According to theory, there is a finite but very small probability that this tiny region could inflate just the way our universe inflated.

Actually, it probably isn't necessary for us to create a region in space that resembles the conditions of the Big Bang. It may be going on around us all the time without our lifting a finger.

There is conclusive experimental evidence that ordinary

empty space is not empty at all. Space on the submicroscopic scale is teeming with quantum fluctuations in energy and density that might well, for an instant, resemble the conditions of a Big Bang. But this instant would be more than enough time for the start and inflation of a new universe.

Would this inflation blow us out of our own universe? No. The equations show that, from our point of view, all we would see is a tiny black hole, which, as we have seen earlier, is a kind of knot in space and time. If we could somehow step out of our universe, we would see this knot bulging out and expanding during the inflationary period into a new universe and then separating from our universe much as a soap bubble from a bubble pipe expands and then disconnects from the pipe to float off on its own, as the figure shows.

NEW UNIVERSE

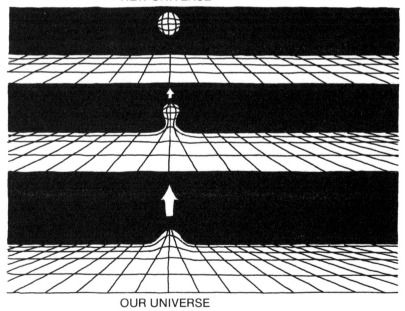

OUR UNIVERSE

Should we take all of this seriously? Well, no one took seriously the prediction of general relativity that the universe must expand, or that mass could be turned into energy, or that there was relic radiation left over from the Big Bang, and so on and on. But for now the reader's guess is probably as good as anyone's. It may well be, however, that the biggest part of our invisible universe is the part that gives birth to new universes every day in our own backyard. It has been said that no creature is less conscious of water than a fish.

Glossary

Absorption line • A dark line superimposed on the continuous spectrum.

Big Bang • The explosive beginning of the universe about 15 billion years ago.

Binary star • A pair of stars revolving around each other.

Blackbody • A material that absorbs and reemits all radiation falling upon it.

Bohr atom • A model of the atom, proposed by Niels Bohr, in which the electrons circle the nucleus in certain allowed orbits.

Boson • One of the fundamental forces carrying particles.

Calibrate • To compare one's measurements to a standard.

Chromosphere • The part of the solar atmosphere just above the sun's surface.

Corona • The sun's outer atmosphere.

Cosmic rays • Charged particles impacting Earth from a source beyond Earth.

Doppler shifts • The apparent change in frequency of radiation due to the relative motion between the observer and the source of the radiation.

Electromagnetic radiation • A wave consisting of oscillating magnetic and electric fields. Examples are light waves, radio waves, and gamma rays.

Electron • A negatively charged particle that circles the nucleus of an atom.

Emission line • A bright line superimposed on the continuous spectrum.

Fermions • The fundamental particles that make up the material universe.

Frequency • The vibration rate of a wave—usually the frequency of an electromagnetic wave, in this book.

Galaxy • A large collection of stars, our Milky Way galaxy, for example.

Gamma rays • The most energetic form of electromagnetic radiation.

General theory of relativity • A theory proposed by Albert Einstein that explains gravity in terms of the geometry of space.

Gravitation • The attraction of matter to other matter.

Infrared ray • A form of electromagnetic radiation at frequencies just below the red end of the visible spectrum of light.

Interstellar medium • The place where the sun's solar wind becomes so weak that it is overcome by stellar winds from other stars.

Kinetic energy • The energy of motion of a body.

Lepton • One of the particles in the family of fermions. Electrons and neutrinos are examples.

Light-year • The distance traveled by light in a year.

Magellanic Clouds • Two groups of stars visible to the naked eye in the Southern Hemisphere.

Neutrino • A subatomic particle with no electric charge that interacts very little with other matter.

Neutron • A subatomic particle with no electric charge.

Neutron star • A very compact star composed almost entirely of neutrons.

Nova • A star that temporarily releases a sudden burst of radiation, increasing its brightness about one thousand times.

Nucleus • The massive central part of an atom about which the electrons revolve.

Olbers' paradox • The paradox of why the sky is not bright both day and night.

Photons • The discrete particles that make up electromagnetic waves.

Planck's radiation theory • How the brightness of a blackbody varies with frequency and temperature.

Proton • A heavy, positively charged particle.

Pulsar • A star that emits pulses of electromagnetic radiation.

Quantum (plural: quanta) • A discrete packet of energy—a photon of light, for example.

Quark • One of the particles in the family of fermions. Quarks are the building blocks of protons and neutrons, for example.

Radiation • The process of emitting energy in the form of electromagnetic waves.

Radio astronomy • The branch of astronomy where observations are made of radio waves.

Red giant • A large, cool star.

Solar wind • A stream of electrically charged particles given off by the sun.

Spectrum • The distribution of energy in an electromagnetic wave according to frequency. A prism, for example, displays the rainbow spectrum of sunlight.

Strong nuclear force • The force that binds the particles in the nucleus together.

Supernova • A stellar outburst where the star's brightness increases by a million times or more.

Ultraviolet ray • A form of electromagnetic radiation whose frequency is just above the violet end of the visible spectrum.

Weak nuclear force • The force in the nucleus of an atom that is responsible for the atom decaying into other kinds of atoms.

White dwarf • A star that has exhausted all of its thermonuclear fuel and has shrunk to about the size of Earth.

X ray • An energetic form of electromagnetic radiation.

For Further Reading

Ferris, Timothy. *The Red Limit: The Search for the Edge of the Universe.* New York: William Morrow, 1977. An excellent elementary introduction to recent developments in astronomy.

Harrison, Edward. *Darkness at Night: A Riddle of the Universe.* Cambridge, MA: Harvard University Press, 1987. A book devoted almost entirely to the historical and scientific aspects of Olbers' paradox.

Jespersen, James, and Jane Fitz-Randolph. *From Quarks to Quasars: A Tour of the Universe.* New York: Atheneum, 1987. A popular introduction to modern physics and its implications for the birth and evolution of the universe.

Kaufmann, William J., III. *Universe.* New York: W. H. Freeman, 1987. A comprehensive book on astronomy for the advanced reader.

Kippenhahn, Rudolph. *Light from the Depths of Time.* Berlin, NY: Springer-Verlag, 1987. A book focusing on modern astronomical observations and theory for the advanced reader.

———. *100 Billion Stars.* New York: Basic Books, 1983. A book at the intermediate level on the birth, death, and evolution of stars.

Tauber, Gerald E. *Man and the Cosmos.* New York: Greenwich House, 1982. A comprehensive history of astronomy from the early Stone Age astronomers to the present.

Index